Praise for Nthikeng Mohlele's *The Scent of Bliss*

'Debut of elusive, skewed beauty.'
– CHRIS DUNTON, *SUNDAY INDEPENDENT*

*'A poetic, vividly imagined, nuanced text, a rare
butterfly in modern African literature.'*
– LIZZY ATTREE, *WORDSETC*

*'An outstanding poetic piece of work ... Mohlele's
voice is novel and shows a concern ... for beautiful
language for its own sake.'*
– PERCY ZVOMUYA, *MAIL & GUARDIAN*

*'An assured debut by a writer who wields his pen
with flair and confidence.'*
– ARJA SALAFRANCO, *THE STAR TONIGHT*

Small Things

Nthikeng Mohlele

First published in 2013 by University of KwaZulu-Natal Press

This edition published by Jacana Media (Pty) Ltd in 2018
Second impression 2019

10 Orange Street
Sunnyside
Auckland Park 2092
South Africa
+2711 628 3200
www.jacana.co.za

ISBN 978-1-4314-2663-8

Cover design by publicide
Set in Sabon 11/14.5pt
Printed and bound by ABC Press, Cape Town
Job no. 003650

See a complete list of Jacana titles at www.jacana.co.za

For
My teacher, LB Mashiane at
St Bede's High School – Mpedi!
My son, Lehlogonolo Mohlele
– Moupo Mokganyammele ...
My friend, Malose Lekganyane
– Kgomo Mohwaduba.

'I am the organiser of the universe and very bossy.
From my right hand issue planets.
From my left hand issue stars.
I have to see that everything stays in order
and the planets do not collide with the stars.
When something threatens order and peace
then I get mad as hell.
But an organiser is not a dictator.
An organiser takes care of everything.'

– BESSIE HEAD, IN THUNDER BEHIND HER EARS,
GILLIAN STEAD EILERSEN

'For all our conceits about being the centre of the
universe, we live in a routine planet of a humdrum
star stuck away in an obscure corner ... on an
unexceptional galaxy, which is one of about 100
billion galaxies ... That is the fundamental fact of
the universe we inhabit, and it is very good for us to
understand that.'

– CARL SAGAN

Life

I, in my own determined and peculiar ways, to certain approximate and exact degrees, don't think much of life. I am, however, never sure if this conclusion is without some blemish, some residue, however faint, of an ounce of madness. To certain inconclusive degrees, it is clear that some of my disappointments awaited me, gathering rust, years before I was born. I have reason to suspect you will find this tale unusual, but not without beauty. Threads of a spider's web perhaps, to be unwound, cautiously, a skein at a time.

1

I, to this day, fall hopelessly in love whenever I see postmen carrying mailbags. My heart leaps at bright-red post boxes in pictures. They remind me of Desiree – the postmaster's daughter. We never exchanged much, Desiree and I. I caught her roving eye on me one morning during Mass. Hearing nothing of the sermon, I saw only this eye, a beaming light bulb that warmed me from the third row, a good twenty metres from where I knelt praying, my knees molten with love.

Seeing her absent-minded, in the company of tedious friends, aroused suspicions that I was in her thoughts. End of term, after the mid-year exams, was marked by forced labour. We cleaned the school grounds and windows in preparation for a new school term. I never joined the gardening or chalkboard-cleaning crews, but always chose to be on the window-cleaning teams, where I could, with good perspective from standing on upside-down dustbins, admire my Desiree shining classroom floors. I got generous compliments from inspecting teachers (windows shone like mirrors against the sun) – who little knew that such workmanship was done in a trance. I was like a spider on a damaged web, doing my utmost to contain my blossoming heart.

It never made sense to me why we had to endure two weeks' break between school terms – during which I almost turned red with longing. My Desiree would, when my hopes were at their highest, at the fast-advancing first day of the new term, come down with swollen tonsils. This I learnt through considered and disciplined interviews with her friends – slippery and non-committal, like goldfish dodging intruding human hands in ponds. Desiree came back to school (a week of absence!) following the tonsils assault, offered me an orange during lunch. She then woke up brave one morning, handed me a sky-blue homemade card that at first appeared blank. But as I opened it, with the care demanded by heart transplants, I learnt she had drawn a small heart at the centre. Complete with a faint fingerprint and candle wax (a confirmation of feelings known and treasured). Executed in candlelight. This awoke the poet in me. I, the same evening, penned a love note whose fire assailed the heart. I wrote: 'My love is deeper than one million seas, brighter than a billion suns, bathed in milk, fanned with tulip bunches. Shared in moderation, for fear of total combustion. Desiree. Desiree. Desiree. Come to my heart. A universe of joy. Lit by a trillion moons.' I never got a response. She would be moody and aloof.

She then promised me eternal love – 'When the time is right'. There were times when I was angry and rebellious; yet helpless. I wrote, in yet another carefully worded love letter, that it was unjust that I had to endure such blissful suffering. I never got a response. Desiree was again down with tonsils, away from school for two weeks, which seemed like eight millennia. She never encouraged my pursuit of her, nor did she discourage it. She seemed undecided, bordering on confused. Not all was covered in soot, though. There were moments when Desiree ignited hushed conversations, only too brief to allow me a glimpse of her torturous charms. It is peculiar, I know, but even now, I associate tonsils with love. In hindsight, my love for Desiree is as it always was: maddening. I visited Desiree at the post office, licked hundreds of stamps on letters to imaginary people. I mopped supermarket floors on weekends, ran errands, to earn money to give impetus to my suit. I bought small things; with big intentions. Wrist watches. Earrings. Tonsil prescriptions.

She appreciated the efforts, yet dismissed them as heart-warming but unnecessary. It took me time to learn her emotional compass – which often spun out of control. I hung on, learnt and unlearnt bizarre discoveries, reassuring compromises, brutal rebukes. I could recognise Desiree's singing or laughter in a hall full of people; even if there was a thunderstorm. She knew this, and I suspect it meant a lot to her. That was why I once inquired if she ever thought of me, to which she, with fire in her eyes, countered: 'What do I have to do for you to leave me alone?' I was beyond bliss. The rebuke was a step in the right direction. Preferable to her more direct protests, the famous: 'Stop staring at me!'

I was born in Sophiatown, the Chicago of South Africa. Benevolence Place was, the day Truman bombed Hiroshima, converted into a Catholic sanctuary for abandoned, orphaned souls, of which I was one. A popular rumour says my father, a contract miner in pursuit of gold, died in a blasting accident. No one knows for sure. I never met my mother. I grew and was schooled around monks, who were quick to say tersely: 'You do not have parents.' Benevolence Place was the only world I knew: Crosses. Church bells. Hymns. Orphans. Our heads were shaved, our existence timed, our opinions disregarded.

Father Goebbels assured me there was no greater relief than unburdening, humbling oneself before the Lord. It puzzled me that he always picked on me, kept nudging me to go for confession. To be one with Christ. I was curious, hesitant, non-committal. I thought: why would Father Goebbels think me guilty of such sordid sins at primary school as to warrant emergency confessions? It took Desiree, accusing me of heathen tendencies, to make me finally relent. I untied knot after knot of my secret worlds: the meat and left-over food heists at Benevolence Place kitchens; peeping at urinating monks. A selection of lies told in no particular sequence. To make life easier. My confessions to Father Goebbels were mostly made up. Mild sins. To get him off my back. The confessions never included my nocturnal escapes to Gold Street, to spy and listen to wails of drunken pleasure in the dark. Lord bless that whorehouse, with its varied paying errands: 'Call Lucy for me, say it is Wilfred.' Sixpence for errands, four pence for spying. I sinned. For Desiree. For love.

'Ask for God's forgiveness then, my son,' said Father Ben. I was, all along, convinced I was talking to God Himself. But the voice, of a sombre yet amused Father Ben, hiding behind the confession box, caused me untold embarrassment every time our paths crossed. Each time Father Goebbels said: 'God loves *all* his children,' I asked, irritated: 'Doesn't God ever tire of hearing the same prayers over and over again?' Father Goebbels warned me against such erratic thinking and, visibly annoyed, said everything has its place in the universe. 'Don't be like your people, bowing to dead things in search of salvation. Don't engage in satanic rituals, drumming to evil spirits. Refrain from lust, voodoo and greed, and from polygamy. Why does a man need three wives, if not to satisfy base, wild instincts? Jesus – only He is the way, the truth and the life.' John 14:6. If everything indeed belonged somewhere, I pondered, why was Desiree blind to my adoration of her? Why did Jesus allow such persecution?

Father Goebbels expected us to do odd jobs in return for sanctuary: remove weeds from flower beds, collect and distribute mail, ring the church bell on general and specific occasions. I was a captive of that bell, in all kinds of weather. I imagine the bell grew tired of me, as I did of it. All Father Goebbels needed to do was frown, and I knew. I would run to the tower, yank that rope to the deafening din announcing Mass or afternoon prayers. I ran in for Mass, rang the bell again to mark the end of prayers. It was only then that

I was free – yet under Father Goebbels's eagle eye, his sour smiles.

For reasons known only to him, Father Goebbels concluded I was never to be trusted with anything. Not even removing weeds from the vegetable gardens, or remembering to ring that wretched bell. There was always his hostile eye, his lemon smiles, following me around. He was creepy: like an uninvited, cynical mortician at a wedding reception. The Dutch, said Father Goebbels, came to the Cape in 1652, to establish a refreshment station. To save sailors bound for the East from scurvy. Such simple-minded fools. Why endure the wrath of the sea, risk losing your teeth and drowning, for a few bags of spice? Father Goebbels refused to answer why most black people I knew shone floors, dug furrows ... a life of servitude. He exploded, catching the class unawares: 'Why don't you stand the hell up and come teach this class then?' I sat still, petrified.

Sophiatown was myriad heartaches: souls stabbed in dark alleys, covered with newspapers and flies come morning. Police lining loitering people up against police vans, frisking them, demanding answers to petty things. Pass books. Places of employment. Lodgings. Intended destinations. The Americans and the Spoilers, mob figures, cruised the streets with their maroon and cream Oldsmobiles and picked unwilling beauties up off dance floors. Like one picks cherries off a birthday cake.

Yet you heard staccato and other breeds of laughter. Midnight wails, too. How was it that amid open sewage, such laughter was possible? That self-taught pianists, painters, writers and unassuming philosophers saw and expressed life with such devastating clarity? It was as if skulls were not being cracked with batons, torches not shone on naked lovers during planned and impromptu raids. Happiness, I found, was a strange creature. While the gramophones wailed, while wedding songs filled romantic summer nights, rumours abounded that Sophiatown would be demolished.

Drunks in the streets sang and stumbled down Gold Street (shebeens, brothels, dagga dens), their jollity interspersed by moments of clouded introspection. I endured Father Goebbels's lemon smiles; until I grew pubic hairs, expressed the most ungodly sentiments I could dream of. I was kicked out of the orphanage, accused of being a demon. My youth was, upon leaving Benevolence Place, consumed by a single urge: to charm Desiree. My night prowlings were never about blowing air onto feminine navels, but lonely hours spent in the Odin Cinema or Back of the Moon. Like a stray dog. In search of not food, but meaning. I hung out with Bra Todd, a respected newsman, with a taste for American swing. 'Everyone is a politician,' he growled, with his infectious laughter. We listened to records, while I polished his shoes, helped with the dishes, and learnt sophisticated ways to woo a lady. I was terrified to let my feelings be known, so although

Bra Todd looked out for me, I refrained from burdening him with my Desiree misfortunes. He was her uncle and, as such, had full command of her attention. How I envied him! I, at fifteen, between bouts of pleading with Desiree (silent, helpless despair), spent many late nights with Bra Todd in newsrooms, as a willing apprentice.

I spent most Sundays at the Odin Cinema, enthralled by competing ensembles: dancers, jazz bands and choral music. Desiree sang for the Fleeting Birds, a group that specialised in church tunes. I, like a man possessed, shuffled between bodies in the overcrowded performance hall, for a view of her. Desiree was always the last to walk on stage, and my sanity momentarily escaped me every time she sang the lead in 'Amazing Grace'. Everyone agreed that the grace was truly amazing – and so was the line of suitors. I made sure I pleased Bra Todd; knew that none of those rascals with pulsating hearts would dare to touch my Desiree. Desiree and I had an understanding, fraught though it was; raging love torrents received with lukewarm courtesy.

Her voice, rising through the performance hall, assured all that God would one day take a stroll through Sophiatown and, as Father Goebbels was fond of saying, 'set the crooked paths straight'. Bra Todd loved Desiree who, in his estimation, had the subtle charms of a fleeting breeze. He would play Louis Armstrong records, his favourite being 'Kiss to Build a Dream On'. I embraced my role of accidental houseboy – for its proximity to Desiree. It never mattered what was thrown my way: cleaning muddy boots, scraping burnt casserole dishes, or the occasional debt-collection voyages – complete with Bra Todd's warnings: 'Tell Joel I have only anger to express.' I loved seeing grown men shiver, mumble incoherent explanations. I collected debts as old as three years – where some debtors suffered bloody noses even after paying in full. I was, by comparison, the safest citizen in Sophiatown. Those in the know would simply say: 'That is Todd's boy, stay clear of him.'

2

The demolition rumour proved to be true. I watched as government lorries moved human cargo; observed Meadowlands, Soweto, sprawl into a majestic, flamboyant eyesore. A place of explosive cocktails of despair, possibilities, limitations. For me, there was something more devastating in the move to Meadowlands: Desiree went to live with her uncle in Alexandra Township; sparking in me sporadic fits of rage that left me drained and ill tempered.

From an Indian shop in Mayfair I bought a second-hand Remington with a faulty ink ribbon that I had to nudge into position every three sentences. My ponderings became letters to the editor, evolved into seething opinion pieces, ending in an offer for a column a few years later. Bra Todd's cautions were clear: 'We love the venom, but tone it down. Or you are as good as a corpse.' It was impossible, having venom I couldn't use, of which I was permitted to emit only small doses. The Venom Debates became explosive newsroom outbursts, ending with surly resignations like: 'Suit yourself; it's your life.' The worst was when Bra Todd simply ignored me. I knew: tone it down.

Just because you do not take an interest in politics doesn't mean politics won't take an interest in you, says Pericles. 495–429 BC or thereabouts. I remember the piece vividly, copied out with a blunt pencil from a maroon leather-bound book, overdue by several days, making the librarians furious. I well recall that book: its coffee stains, the faded gold lettering proclaiming *Greek Philosophers*, the dead cockroach with its abandoned wing on page 322 and the rest of its corpse and crushed antennae preserved on page 548.

I took a walk to the *Daily Argus* entrance below, shared the contents of my lunchbox with eager pigeons, jostling for the best position next to my charitable hand. The sun cast gold light spells on the newsroom windows. An assortment of cars was dotted around the parking lot under the yellow afternoon light: Cadillacs. Valiants. Oldsmobiles. Constancias.

The weather changed without warning. A gloomy, tempestuous storm stalked the cityscape. It hit Johannesburg sooner than anticipated, dropping nipple-sized hailstones. Palm trees in city parks bowed obediently to God's invisible hand. Wind blew water against window panes, causing blurry vision. Bad-tempered lightning and sudden thunder bullied the senses.

I rushed back into the newsroom, just in time to catch a phone call. 'Bastards!' said Bra Todd. 'You are on the list.' I was not surprised. A yellow Ford Cortina had tailed me for some weeks. The vehicle occupants, weird-looking men with sweaty armpits, following me around, tapping my phone, making me nervous. My indifference to my pending arrest intrigued them. How was it that I continued with my blighted routines, as if there were no noose dangling over my head? I risked working late. The 10:00 pm curfew was simple: no African permitted on the streets – your desires and tragedies notwithstanding. I spent my thirty-third birthday transfixed behind my desk. Thinking.

I arrived home at dawn. The yard was swarming with police vehicles. My heart thundered. My throat was aflame with helpless fear. The house was being ransacked, sniffer dogs led to cupboards, intruding into every imaginable space. There was dog hair on my towels, my bedding, my cheap curtains. I asked politely what the commotion was about – to which a uniformed figure advised: 'Do not interfere with lawful police business, Kaffir.' Though the officers were mostly polite and though they explained very little, their sombre search suggested there was something great at stake. The team leader, who had ignored me thus far, introduced himself as Major Joubert. Lead investigator. 'You have to come with me. Answer a few questions,' he said.

'Who exactly are you looking for?'

'You. Come with me. To that Ford by the gate.'

I froze. Major Joubert's terseness hinted at agitation: 'To the car, please.'

No handcuffs. No explanations. No force. I was warned: stop your nonsense. *Of dan gaan jy kak* (or you're going to shit yourself). There was no further talk. Major Joubert signalled and his officers slowly shuffled out, torch beams still bouncing onto the walls, the coal box. Soweto was graveyard silent.

I penned an article, all of three thousand words, 'State of Neurosis', the next morning. It was published on the front page of the *Daily Argus*, sparking furious anonymous support letters to the editor. I walked home to Soweto three days later, after killing time in the newsroom, to find Major Joubert's yellow Ford parked at the gate. He looked at me, lit a cigarette, shook his head in pity and disbelief. He, before throwing me handcuffs, said: 'You put me in a very awkward situation, Che.'

I sighed. 'What is the charge?'

The four detectives accompanying him stirred against the walls. He shook his head, commanded: 'Let's go.'

I was blindfolded, driven to Republic House, an infamous interrogation facility nestled on a hill, hidden behind high security walls, its secrets further entombed in intricate foliage. The amount of questions I was asked generated enough paperwork to cremate an average-sized corpse – yet there seemed to be no end in sight. The questions kept coming, in different guises, alternating tempos. None of the documentation explicitly bore my name or related to me in any way.

Days and nights dragged by. Midnight interrogation sessions were mostly about specific poets and editors – whom Major Joubert accused me of knowing and, worse, sharing treasonous pursuits with. He was irritable, often dejected, and without doubt disillusioned by his interrogation crusade. There were obvious lapses in judgement on his part, in the way some questions seemed designed to pass time rather than establish deep-set treason.

Major Joubert poured me coffee, explaining why justice was such a slippery slope; why it was, for a selection of people, necessary to follow long processes, weed out any contradictions, in pursuit of justice, in its purest form. He said it sometimes meant that things were left as they were. That did not mean there was an absence of justice or guilt, but that the purity thereof was in doubt. In such cases, he said, fixing me with a stare, even treasonous rogues are set free. Guilt, he said, like truth, does not end with establishing the facts, understanding the motivations, confirming and apportioning blame. Philosophical, that Major Joubert. I protested: 'If you are going to line me up against the wall with a firing squad, do it quickly. I have no time for your theatrics.' The major simply shook his head, stifled a yawn with the back of his hand. A skinny man of average build, clean-shaven, with a pleasant smile; more suited for packing watermelons and tomatoes in supermarkets than hunting down rebels. He looked at me, a gentle smile playing on his ruby lips, and said: 'I have all the time in the world. The question is: do you? Thousands have sat in the exact same chair as you, answering and dodging the exact questions being put to you. Look, I have a comfortable bed, three adorable German Shepherds, a wife who abhors me as Adolf Hitler risen from the dead. Can you believe it? We can end this thing and go home. It is up to you.'

My 'misguided insolence', as he termed it, caused me several years in solitary confinement. I was driven around farms in rusty labour lorries, broke my back digging potatoes under police guard. The routine was predictable: ten hours under lock and key and practically every waking minute digging furrows, clearing bushes, moving and carrying logs and timber. My body ached. I longed for the comfort of the newsroom, the park pigeons, Bra Todd's gramophone. What wounded me most was not the back-breaking work but being commanded to do things against my will. And the food! Stale bread and jam that tasted like motor grease. You could not feign sickness, and everyone in the work groups – condemned men fished from Johannesburg prisons, accused of the most imaginary crimes – knew you had to have your bowels hanging out of your anus to be even remotely considered sick. We mixed mortar on construction sites, chopped truckloads of wood for God knew which furnaces, dug graves and buried paupers, pruned trees wherever such a need arose. We developed friendships, learnt of appalling accusations, laughed heartily at our misery.

1976 seemed like nine years folded into one – tense and unpredictable. A skew friendship blossomed between Major Joubert and I, away from the guards on the watchtowers. We, on some occasions, spoke through my cell window. By his own admission, Major Joubert was not sentimental. He had no ear for music but was a great admirer of explosives instead. Cesaria Evora, Sarah Vaughan, meant nothing to him. He dreamt of leaving the police force one day, to try his hand at farming. Vineyards. 'Farming and music go together,' I warned him, 'for both depend on some dose of grace, of patience. It is not quite like digging rifle butts into the ribs of people. Grapes can't be scared into blossoming.' My guidance was not heeded. 'What is this Soweto nonsense, kids burning their schools, clinics then?' A beat. 'Do you want kids with their brains on the tarmac? Have you any idea how bad that makes us look? Will you take responsibility for the loss of lives?'

Major Joubert was indifferent during 1977, irritated by my persistent silence. 'It is not that bad. All you need do is tell me who you are working for. Why this obsession to embarrass the Republic? We are not against newspapers. We take exception to crude opinions, to aspirant revolutionaries. To seeds of public unrest.' He looked into my eyes, tapping the interrogation room table with his knuckles. Then, as if overwhelmed by being the bearer of bad news, said: 'Steve Biko is dead. He was arrested at a roadblock outside King William's Town, outside of his banning area.' He lit a cigarette. 'A hunger strike. Well, some scuffle with the police, but nothing serious. Poisonous, that Biko.' He signalled to the guards on the watchtowers, clasping automatic rifles, dozing to breaking news on squeaky transistor radios. I heard a truck drive off as I eased myself onto the chair. I thought: confinement. Under vast blue skies, surrounded by blooming foliage. Beautiful.

Major Joubert came back at the crack of dawn, with more news from home: Bra Todd had died. He endured broken ribs and blue eyes, retelling the same truth: that he never had discussed any revolution with me. That our late-night sessions at the newsroom were of a personal nature. Nothing more. He was dragged out of the newsroom to undisclosed locations, beaten to a pulp. Mauled by police hounds. Submerged under water. Electrocuted. Yanked by the testicles. A similar fate, said Major Joubert, awaited me. 'Stop this obsession with martyrdom. Just tell the truth. Who are your accomplices? No man is an island. Don't be a martyr. For what? To get a hospital, an orphanage named after you? Turn state witness. Tell me something. Anything. Don't be a hero. Then we set you free. It is that simple. Silence is dangerous in our world.'

Yet I chose silence. Served my time, every bruising millisecond, threats of imminent hanging ringing in my ears.

It is true. My flirtations with newspapers had allowed me glimpses into certain secrets: that the Freedom Charter would be signed weeks before there was a whisper of it in Soweto. I sat in midnight meetings in obscure Johannesburg locations; received handwritten notes, scribbled jottings about imminent bus boycotts. Rumours that there would be a march in Sharpeville. I never anticipated corpses strewn across dusty streets, their hearts and skulls blown to oblivion. Yet, unlike Bra Todd and others, I survived. Pruned trees. Dug furrows. Buried paupers.

Nausea

3

My freedom seems like a mockery of all things decent. I had come to accept I was destined to die in detention, with a guaranteed pauper's funeral. I am shocked by the angst of chasing the memory of Johannesburg. Eighteen years of separation has made things and faces unfamiliar, simmering with a daunting sweet-bitterness – like a cancelled march to the gallows. My destiny remains written in the stars. I have to survive. For Desiree. Even if it is only for an hour, a minute ... for glimpsing a shadow of her walking in the moonlight. A scent of hers. Anything.

Vandals have played havoc with my modest home. Years of neglect, and fate, ensured the yard is now a thriving flower shop belonging to a deaf Mozambican cobbler. All his paperwork, citizenship included, confirms he is the rightful owner of 284 Hope Street, Meadowlands.

I sleep in city squares, bath in public toilets. The pigeons know me by name now – but they are too busy competing for breadcrumbs to converse about life and its limits. I am, in their company, alone to admire the many types of knees belonging to mini-skirted beauties fishing for life companions and fuck-mates in the alluring evening light of the city precincts.

Distant giggles (clandestine love affairs) and cutlery sounds from an array of nearby Mediterranean and African restaurants provide the ambience. I examine myself: faultless jaw line; a smile that has, once in a while, disrobed giggly beauties; a well-formed torso; handsome face; eyebrows rich-textured, with a modest shine; and eyes that put planets to shame.

Years pass, with no discernible change in my fortunes. I am drawn to the Nelson Mandela Bridge, linking Newtown and Braamfontein, dignified under its white and blue lights. I run my hand along the pedestrian railing, my eyes collecting known sights: idle trains and gleaming railway lines below; late-night workers running for taxis and safety; beggars draped in plastic and grime. A truck ferrying street sweepers in orange overalls roars past, as bridge lights dazzle moths. A Dark Figure walks from Braamfontein in the direction of the city centre; the leisurely walk of a loner content with life. I marvel at the postcard view of Johannesburg, its fusion of lights, the illusion of cosmopolitan prosperity, admire the deceptions of the cityscape, the elaborate highways, the skyscrapers and horizons painted enchanting hues by God and pollution. Speeding cars glide along the M1 South highway, to Soweto and other destinations. The M1 North, in the opposite direction, snakes past Melrose Arch, Woodmead, Midrand and Centurion, to Pretoria and its surrounds. A chilly evening breeze bites my nostrils. I muse on youth dying predictable deaths; on souls in transition, each suckling at the city's varied breasts for survival. The Dark Figure is now a few paces away. His jeans hang halfway down his buttocks. He wears a red tracksuit top, sports an Afro, with a Jimi Hendrix-type hat concealing his face.

'Share some smoke with a nigger,' he says, without greeting.

'I don't smoke.'

'No shit. You don't smoke?'

A jet thunders overhead, majestic in the night sky. 'Why don't you smoke?'

'I just don't,' I say, getting agitated.

The Dark Figure thinks long and hard, finally says: 'Sorry-ass motherfucker. So you think you are better than me?'

'No.'

'You a priest or something, man?'

'No. A former prisoner.'

'No shit. What the problem was?'

'Say again?'

'Why did they jail your ass?'

'For nothing.'

'How long?'

'Eighteen years.'

'Nigger, please. Eighteen years, and you ain't done shit? Spineless son a bitch. Why the fuck should you continue living, fool?'

'Because I am a good man.'

'So I am a bad man now, huh? Good man my ass. Fuck that shit. You ain't shit.'

The Dark Figure pulls a gun. 'Hook a nigger with some Benjamins.'

'Say again?'

'Some paper, motherfucker, money!'

'I am unemployed.'

'Don't make me shoot you, man, I ain't playing with your stupid ass!'

I snap: 'What gives you the right to insult me?'

A shot rings out, tears through my stomach. The Dark Figure smiles. Such beautiful teeth. Another bullet grazes my groin, and a third shatters my big toe. I clutch my stomach, oozing with warm, sticky, foamy blood. I feel cold, light-headed. I collapse onto the bridge rail, feel my life slowly drain away. Something about the gunshots is marvellous: the deafening explosions, the flash of angry blue flame, the intoxicating smell of gunpowder. Those seconds, time between the shots, the tense moments of unpredictable consequences, are the closest one gets to a God experience – that complete tranquillity of a brutalised body numbed of all feeling, as the Dark Figure aims his gun with random abandon. My fading mind feeds me enchanting views of the Nelson Mandela Bridge, of the city, unlike any other spot in the temptress flirt that is Johannesburg. This unforgiving concrete thing. I marvel at the furious and arty cloud formations, the breathtaking hues of fiery pinks and moody greys.

I hear the Dark Figure light a cigarette, smell nicotine, hear him shuffle away. Blood drains from my wounds onto the concrete, bathed in blue and white light. Late trains pull into Park Station below, their coaches drumming a choochoo rhythm. I think: what a beautiful way to die. To a rhythm. I finally admit to myself: Desiree never loved me. She pitied me, maybe, but it was never love. I also, my soul ensnared in barbed wire, admit that her rebuffs, her barking at me, did not dent the purity of my love; for it continued, like termites, to chew at my soul, leaving me perpetually light-headed and on the verge of weeping.

Two policemen visit me, two weeks after I was shot. I'm told I am in Auckland Park, at the Milpark Hospital. The bullets have missed vital organs, and I am lucky to be alive, a Dr Moodley informs me. I am shown three identikits by Inspector Matros, a chubby, chocolate-skinned, dimpled police officer of modest sensuality. Not ugly, not beautiful, but of average, tolerable looks. She asks after my well-being, before switching to official police business.

'Are any of these men the one who shot you?'

I squint. She walks closer to the bedside, pictures of suspected thugs in her hand. I don't answer.

'This one, maybe?' I shake my head. None of the pictures are monster-looking at all – though Inspector Matros's colleague, Detective Govender, confirms the men in them are deadly fugitives. Armed robberies. Murder. Daring fraud. Yet they look nothing like murderous robbers with fraudulent tendencies but, rather, average altar boys, commanded by spiritual obedience. Ice-cream vendors. Petty pick-pockets maybe. But murderers? A tube is pushed into my side, drains the phlegmy, clotted blood. Breathing is laborious, coughing torturous, laughing brutally painful.

'Beautiful teeth. The man who shot me had lovely teeth,' I tell them.

'Can you describe him?' asks Detective Govender.

'No. It was night. He had a Jimi Hendrix hat over his head.' Inspector Matros frowns: 'Anything else, besides the teeth?'

'No.'

'A statement will help us with opening an official docket and launching an investigation – you know, laying formal charges,' says the modestly sensual one.

'I have nothing to say. If you find him, good; if not, that is also fine with me.'

'This devil nearly took your life, almost put you in a wheelchair!' says Detective Govender, visibly agitated.

I sneeze. The pain tears through my wounds, leaving me on the brink of bellowing. I take a deep breath.

'Yes. But I am not dead, neither am I in a wheelchair.'

'So you are not pressing charges?' asks the dimpled one.

'I take a philosophical view of these things. So, no.'

Exasperation. Irritation. Bewilderment.

There are chimes from the hospital hallways, announcing an end to visiting hours. Dr Moodley returns, advises that I should be left alone to rest. Inspector Matros and her accomplice shuffle out, taking their thug photo gallery with them. I doze off into deep, magnetic sleep.

I am woken at seven: dinner and medication time.

A nurse hands me pain tablets, wheels in a beeping machine to record 'vital signs'. I survive on custard and jelly, following my futile surgery. The bullet eluded the surgeons, though it is 'somewhere inside you'. How do they know that for sure? Easy, they answer: there is no exit wound, which is unusual, given the point-blank range.

I have never thought there is anything wrong with dying. Two of my ward mates are discharged (gall-stone operation, hip fracture), leaving me with the handsome monk admitted with suspected arsenic poisoning. He sleeps all day, adding to the gloom of dreary television programmes: documentaries on Adolf Eichmann but nothing about music; obsession with celebrity carnal scandals but not a word about the purpose of life, of existence. I lie back, listen to my murmuring heart. A heart that has been twitching with profound yet unreachable desires ever since I knelt in that wretched church, my knees molten with love. I mumble my poems from memory; poems about secrets, about moonless nights pierced by trumpet sobs, about obscure things. Dr Moodley clears his throat, readies that soothing baritone of his:

'This is a great country, but fools will ruin it.'

'It's possible.'

'Angry, directionless losers, pissed off with everything. This obsession with hurting others ...' he says.

'It's just a few lost souls.'

A nurse replaces my drip, now drooping like an ageing breast. A veil of silence descends on the ward. Dr Moodley returns, consults the medical file, assures me of a few things: my pulse is good, heart rate steady, blood pressure normal. Anything but normal; I have a pint of a stranger's blood pumped into my veins (blood of a noble soul, I pray ... or of a madman I will never meet). My protestations were dismissed, for 'no one survives with that amount of blood loss'.

I am again visited by the tolerably dimpled one, accompanied by Detective Govender. They ask after my recovery, show me more photographs of suspected thugs. I repeat myself: I am not interested in anything more to do with the Dark Figure, and would rather leave his arrest to diligent police work. It is not obstruction of justice, I tell them, it is how I feel. The law works differently, they warn me.

'He has shot and killed a tourist. Same description, same modus operandi.'

'Regrettable. But what does that have to do with me?'

Inspector Matros stifles a yawn, scratches the back of her neck: 'What did he say was the reason for shooting you?'

I feel drained: 'How should I know? A cigarette, some money.'

'Is that all?'

'Yes.'

'Do you want to add anything?'

'No.'

I think: maybe they will catch him, maybe they won't. Either way, I don't see why I am suddenly expected to be a criminal psychologist.

How do I tell the investigating officers to leave me alone? That I have no interest in chasing ghosts? To my mind, no man should hold the power of life and death over others. But to *his* mind, there are perhaps compelling reasons to murder strangers in cold blood. How can I be expected to know what those reasons are? The Dark Figure had cigarettes. It is possible that he had money, too – the supposed motive for my near-fatal wounds. A chilling hint stands out: he asked me why I should continue living. What answer is expected from souls that face random executioners? I spend days debating with myself: why does the Dark Figure think strangers owe him explanations, obedience? Extreme narcissism, perhaps? Or something more sinister? Murder is supposed to be a conscience-wrecking deed; how was it then that the Dark Figure seemed so composed, without a shred of remorse?

4

I respond to a newspaper advertisement for a temporary job for an Information Officer knowledgeable about 'struggle history' at the Tourism Information Centre in Newtown. I am advanced in age, I am told during the interview. Yet not, it seems, completely useless. My boss is a nosy little irritant with bad breath and nasal speech: Bernadette or Ordette or some such. The job requires little thinking. I simply dish out information brochures and maps to an assortment of tourists. Germans. Japanese. Africans. Canadians. I offer advice on tourism sites, on memorable experiences; how to get to war memorials, to the Apartheid Museum, theme parks, places for period architecture, whorehouses. I speak to bankers, Vietnamese nuns, filmmakers, hungover writers, groupies, necrophiliacs, academics and sweaty backpackers. 'Vilakazi Street, Soweto, is your kind of place. Magalies Meander for walking trails. Nelson Mandela Square for intercontinental cuisine,' I tell them. I think: how does a person endure a fourteen-hour flight, come all the way to South Africa and request to view corpses? Are there no corpses in Yemen, or are foreign ones more appealing? Where does one draw the line between tourism and perversion?

Months pass, with no incident worth noting. What

hope lies in directing perverts where to find illicit pleasures on Jan Smuts Avenue, forbidden fruits loitering around Sandton hotel lobbies (classy hookers clutching counterfeit Gucci handbags, their eyes, their trade, their souls, hidden behind dark Dolce and Gabbana shades bought on street corners)? I, on my free days, to earn extra money, work for a laundry service company: hospital bed linen, full of all manner of stains. I save enough to rent a furnished townhouse at 144 Verona Estates (high-security townhouses of Tuscan design) in Rosebank. The townhouse, the letting agent says, belongs to a Gideon Bemba, a Congolese astronomy professor with ambitions to work for NASA. Gideon is now officially a South African citizen; humble to a fault, with a laser beam for a mind, auctioned to the highest bidders in foreign universities. I miss the city park benches, the nightmares, the occasional erotic dream blended with police sirens and meows from stray cats.

It takes months of reflection, many considered choices, until the study at 144 Verona Estates is adorned with all sorts of time pieces: wall clocks, an array of wrist watches, pendulums. The bookshelves house poets, arranged by country and reputation, according to whether living or dead, in strict alphabetical, colour-coded order. I am not reading for pleasure or to gather knowledge, but simply because I don't know what else to do with myself these days. Philosophy books, African mythology, Greek and Eastern contemplations, flood my bedside – some of which I have spent weeks rummaging through dingy bookstores to find; out-of-print gems. The shelves are also home to an assortment of sea shells for decorative effect. The walls are adorned with pictorial depictions of galaxies, of astronomical puzzles and latest discoveries, arranged by date and significance. Framed, tastefully. Cosmic secrets as wall art, beautiful beyond measure.

I walk to the Nelson Mandela Bridge, to eavesdrop on animated conversations from students and aggrieved workers en route to bus and taxi stations. Except for the occasional loner, the students commute in groups, debating anything from Robert Mugabe to birth control pills. Their talk is laced with sneers against privileged white students whose great grandparents plundered Africa, and Nigerians who are turning Johannesburg into a drug den. From the sound of things, judging by the conversations in motion, the lanky boy in military slacks speaks less, thinks more. The students pause mid bridge, share a cigarette. 'Not all Nigerians are drug lords,' says the lanky one to his overweight companion.

'No flipping Nigerians in South Africa, period. That goes for all the Zimbabweans, Mozambicans, Somalis and Chinese – everyone,' says the fat one.

'Hold it, Thebe,' says the lanky one. 'This is the African Century ...'

'African Century my foot. Aren't there universities in Zimbabwe?'

'Other Africans are people too. Why is it so unthinkable that Nigerians, Mozambicans, Zimbabweans and others should feel our freedom also belongs to them? That it is only fair to demand a little courtesy? What African Century is possible when freedom becomes a brick to crack the skulls of others?'

Thebe laughs mockingly at that. The lanky one dismisses him with an irritable wave of the hand, kills his cigarette under his boot. The conversation subsides into hushed tones, in response to an approaching group of girls – well-sculptured creatures with intricate hairdos, performing their every step as if expecting wolf whistles, savouring the bliss of being watched. They speak not of drug dens, but of the delights of malva pudding. Then suddenly *he* appears! Unmistakable. Those lovely teeth. He wears the red tracksuit with the Jimi Hendrix hat on his head, strides across the bridge with careless abandon. I am amazed how ordinary he looks in daylight; how he, without his gun, blends into African-Century and malva-pudding conversations. I follow him down the bridge in the direction of the city, absorbing every detail: the bouncy walk, the fruity perfume, the cowboy boots. A silver chain hangs from his baggy jeans, dangling in slow motion, as in American music videos. I stalk him downtown with relish and pangs of fear, along busy city streets. As if in Technicolor he glides, he alone the only human, commanding a vast victim's empire that stretches beyond the imagination; occasionally adjusting the tracksuit under which is concealed a weapon, awaiting nightfall. I am nervous yet thrilled. I quicken my pace, walk past him, and turn a corner to retrace my steps towards him for a face-to-face encounter. Sweat pours from my armpits. My steps are brisk but unsteady. Time freezes amid hooting motorists and city sounds. I wave at him the way one acknowledges a nervous child. He smiles, nods in what appears to be profound humility. My gamble pays off; he does not recognise me – or so I assume. Overwhelmingly strange, this feeling of being party to fate.

I turn around and follow the Dark Figure. I walk along renamed streets, a Newtown bearing famous names of the Sophiatown Renaissance. Jazz artists. Painters. Journalists. At Henry Nxumalo Street he takes a left, past Miriam Makeba, and right towards Gwigwi Mgwebi. It seems odd that he takes such a long-winded route home, to the apartments nestled below the Nelson Mandela Bridge. I follow him up a flight of stairs; pause as he enters Apartment 307. I go up an extra flight, take cover under evening shadows for God's view of the apartment below.

A dreary five minutes crawl past, the pulse in my temples throbbing with anticipation. The door of Apartment 307 opens and he (on the cellphone) pulls the door shut, walks away briskly. My eyes follow him down a flight of stairs, to the parking area and out the main gate, until he disappears in the direction of the bridge. I waste no time; in the door, the key is sitting. The simplicity of the apartment's interior is disarming: a defeated mattress on the floor, a few clothes stuffed into a cardboard box, a kettle with newly boiled water. Red underwear hangs on the shower knobs. The bathroom mirror is adorned with spots from minor toothpaste accidents. The wardrobes are bare, except for a broken umbrella, a humble blanket. Such emptiness, such a barren existence. What does he eat?

My heart is pounding. Under the mattress is a mountain-climbing rope, a page from a magazine, on which an elderly woman depicts solitary lust. Cockroach spray is on the stove, next to which are headache tablets. The kitchen cabinets are bare, not even a teaspoon in sight. I stand in the bathroom, considering options to let my presence here be known: the kettle water will wet the mattress just fine. I could put the underwear in the kettle, rub toothpaste on the bathroom mirror. The prospects are exhilarating, the combinations abundant. I do what comes naturally: leave everything as I have found it. Then board a bus back to Verona Estates.

Someone telephones from the Tourism Office to say there are policemen looking for me. I give the address, and half an hour later there is a polite knock on the door. The modestly sensual one is not alone, but not with Detective Govender either; this time it is an Inspector Slabbert with her – a blue-eyed brunette, too cute to be carrying guns and handcuffs. They decline my coffee offer and, once seated, waste no time: 'Three varsity students were gunned down yesterday evening at the bottom end of the bridge. There must be something more that you remember about your tragedy?' Tragedy. It might as well be comedy – being shot for choosing not to smoke. There is so much I could tell them today; yet not much at all. He masturbates to wrinkled porn models; keeps broken umbrellas; suffers from headaches. On condition that I be left alone, I tell them of my visit to Apartment 307, a description so detailed that even I wonder where such painstaking observation came from.

It is true – I had eighteen years to learn the depths, the limits of my own mind. That is what prison does to you: slows down your existence, allows you to hold onto contradictory ideals without one dominating the other. I don't expect the investigating officers to understand the power of rising above one's temperament, of learning not to (without proper reflection) reject brutal infringements, because their interpretation is so slippery. Even now, I sometimes forget I can go wherever I please, for in my mind the world has shrunk, stripped of all sights and sounds, save for a concrete bed and a steel lavatory. Opposed though I am to murder, I also acknowledge I have no divine powers to interpret random acts of violence. What, for instance, draws such a hunk as he to ageing, drooping breasts, to the stained teeth of a wretched life displayed on pornographic magazine pages? The outcome of my disclosure is predictable: the police will make an arrest, lock him up, throw away the key. But that answers nothing.

Inspector Matros looks at me curiously, gathers courage to say: 'I am not trying to be insensitive. But it seems to me that you are not affected by your misfortune.' Tragedy. Misfortune. One and the same thing but not necessarily of equal weight. Misfortune is when you get shot for choosing not to smoke. Tragedy is when you get asked why you should continue living. I look from her to the not-too-bad-to-walk-down-the-aisle Inspector Slabbert, and deflect her question.

'Where is Detective Govender?'

'Shot and killed.'

'I see.'

'Why do you brush all questions about your incident aside?' she presses on.

I am holding the door open for them and don't answer.

'Do you mind if I ask you one last question?' she persists.

'Go ahead.'

'Why did you go to Apartment 307?'

'I wanted to see what death looks like.'

'And?'

'I haven't seen it.'

5

I trace Desiree through Mabel, her distant cousin in Alexandra Township. Mabel confesses she has heard 'many things' about me – tells me not a single day passes without Desiree reminiscing, consumed by what might have been. Thrilled at being the bearer of miraculous news, Mabel arranges a surprise dinner at the Park Hyatt Hotel, where she is Guest Relations Manager. Desiree turns out to be far from what I had expected, married to an overweight mathematician with a missing thumb. I, in the most subtle yet ardent manner, protest that her backtracking on such an old commitment – to grant me her heart – is tantamount to treason. She accuses me of melodrama; states firmly that she owes no one any explanation for what she decides to do with her life. She is a prized asset at Nathan Wallace & Associates, a reputable criminal law firm. In her aloof kind of way, she says simply: 'I met someone. I am married. Amazu is a Nigerian academic, a lamb of a man, sweet to a fault.'

Amazu came to South Africa as a professor of mathematics: numbers and decimal points, things without soul. I met him once or twice, a toad with a head full of numbers, grinning at everyone, drenched in his own sweat. A likeable fellow, if one tries hard enough; bland, though, deaf in one ear, always craning his neck to hear what is being said.

I hate his 'what was that?' mantra, so avoid conversing with him, except for the occasional nod in response to his grinning at me; mistaking me for his friend. But Desiree loves him, has given her heart to him. I think it a cruel game when Desiree, a few months later, declares she is now ready to leave Amazu and move in with me. As long as I promise not to leave plates, crawling with ants, festering in our bed. As long as I flush the toilet after use, understand that snoring is detrimental to romance. That there is much more to the world than trigonometry. And, most important of all, that she is entitled to her temper. God made her so, included a temper of volcanic proportions, and God does not make mistakes. I am delighted. Dumbstruck. Confused. Desiree understands the depth of my emotion, bends and shapes it to suit her whims.

I think: there are many kinds of love. Desiree's is an eloping kind, a love that constructs and abandons nests, much like a fugitive dodging police hounds. How else do I explain such lukewarm, inconsistent sentiments as hers? I receive Desiree's love, rationed, measured, placed on a scale, the excess fat and bones trimmed off, correct reading confirmed. The same way prisoners live on rationed meals, are counted and recounted to detect escapes. Desiree is expert at placing things in boxes, with the right measurements. Her thoughts do not mix with her yearnings; yearnings are separated from obsessions; disappointments removed from ambitions; and secrets boxed away from petty observations and selected erotic lapses. Her mind toils with estimations, discoveries and protests known only to herself. Her lone meditations are marked by profound, often scary, announcements, expressed as statements of fact not open for discussion: 'I don't believe in love.' Objections from me are met with frowns, suspended rage.

Desiree and I spend a lot of time at 144 Verona Estates, which is to say I watch her sleeping, drained from the unpredictable life of a defence attorney. I adore my Desiree: her soaring voice as she sets old jazz standards ablaze; her uplifting voice, accompanied by whispers of steamy shower water. My love for her is still as distinct, detailed and colourful as coral reeds in sea beds. It cannot be said to be ordinary – the way my heart glows and burns with each of her brutal remarks, the way my disappointments leave me frosty yet thawing from the core. Mine is not the kind of love to inspire shallow romantic dramas, for it has, at its heart, a flame that refuses to die.

When she's in a bad mood, Desiree's voice rises and falls with beautiful symphonies in multiple vocal ranges, an assortment of popular rhythm and blues standards, heart-wrenching funeral songs. I know she is begging for forgiveness when her voice begins to quiver, when there are lapses between otherwise straightforward choruses. When she showers for what seems like eternity, followed by many hours of feigned sleep. My own gestures, the granting of that forgiveness, are equally calculated. I offer her tea in bed; volunteer that it will be the television news soon; note down and remind her of personal calls she's missed.

I suffer little irritations, sulking sessions, followed by wounded withdrawals, sealed by bleeding silences and a bellyful of wine and tears. My Desiree, with beautiful armpits and perfect shoulder blades, born without a shred of compassion. I love her and that leaves me drained and mildly suicidal. I read up extensively on various painless methods to get rid of myself: carbon monoxide, or morphine overdose maybe. To die seeing pictures, the sights of a brain under siege – how charming, how beautifully sad.

To some exact degree, I am defenceless against her callous abuse, but to certain approximate degrees, I find that I am trapped in hope that Desiree's temper will one day fade away. There is a kind of radiance lurking deep within her. I can feel the subtle hints, the whispers, implying that, in a way, she does not mean the harm she causes, that she herself is often amazed by her own fury. But how was it that Amazu remained so seemingly unperturbed by her treatment, concerned only with his algebra classes, taught to 'born frees' – Tupac Shakur and Rihanna clones – at the University of the Witwatersrand? What does he know that I don't (all that grinning of his)? Or is it just his mathematical mind, finding logic in infinite possibilities? By the look of things, Amazu is used to disappointments. Embarrassments. Judgements. He volunteered a hint of this once: 'Desiree is a classic case. Bipolar disorder.' Maybe. But then, mathematicians are not physicians. He is not a poet, either. What does he know about love?

Though Desiree insists on calling me her Poodle, I never officially accepted the pet name. Poodle. Imagine! I simply grunt when she lumps me with the dog race. I have no pet name for her either; she is just plain old Desiree to me. She, for no reason, slaps my wandering hand whenever I try to coax her into pleasure rituals. One premeditated excuse after another: headaches; the summer heat; mourning for her departed grandfather, who passed on many years ago. She can read my thoughts, sense my intentions before I even have the time to formulate them. It is not unusual for her to say, out of the blue, when lights are switched off and bodies positioned in preparation for dozing: 'My period has come unexpectedly.'

'Do your periods just drop from the sky, unannounced?'

She fumes: 'Have you no other things to think about?'

'I realise I am courting a stone.'

'You will wish for tender moments, moaning like a camel dying of thirst. Keep talking like someone demented and let's see where that gets you!' she snaps.

There are times when Desiree bursts into tears, without provocation. I blamed it erroneously on her midnight whisky binges; on grief in the wake of a breast cancer misdiagnosis. Not knowing the true cause, I was puzzled at the way Desiree's world fell apart; by the moving eulogy she paid to our childhood yearnings, our sudden love that blossomed and peaked out of nowhere. I was moved by her suffering, her helplessness. My confusion turned to outrage when Desiree, her belly full of enough wine to floor nine pirates, later said: 'I have never believed in love.'

Desiree's temper borders on insanity. I suffer wounding accusations, haunting blackmail. She starts losing cases in court, argues with judges, storms out of courtrooms. She is in the papers – for giving a state prosecutor a bloody nose. The cause: a difference of opinion in the interpretation of law. She is temporarily suspended from the bench, for behaviour unbecoming to a legal mind. She languishes in despair, fuels my gloom with her ferocious rebukes. She leads the evidence: cross-questions me on mundane lapses, turns 144 Verona Estates into a perpetual courtroom. 'I can argue ten reasons why your love of me is brittle,' she says over breakfast. 'Your obsession with me is tantamount to suicide.' I suffer panic attacks these days, kick and toss in my sleep. Our mealtimes are accompanied by mountain ranges of legal papers, filed by myriad law firms. Legal arguments seeking to set rapists free. My Desiree is master at what she does: she plants confusion, engenders doubt in known and accepted things, cross-examines star witnesses until they forget their very names. 'There is no such thing as an unwinnable case,' she asserts. She has corpses exhumed to prove obscure arguments with penetrating precision. 'The law,' says my celebrity lawyer lover, who thrives on courtroom gasps, as she pages through graveyards of legal minefields, 'does not need to be fair. Just as life isn't fair. Everyone knows justice can be bought, that it is a sham. We use technical arguments to undermine truth, unfounded and indefensible probabilities to obscure reason, selective questions to draw inferences, cast doubt on innocent people. The law can prosper without truth. Just as life can exist without love.' Words. A view of life. True, maybe. Detrimental to me, a sentimental soul with poetic ambitions.

Desiree is not a poet but a creature of law, a profession built of opposing and defending things.

6

I take countless bus rides between Rosebank and Newtown. There are times when I think about early separation. Yet I still play the role of lover, comforter. Aside from Desiree, my life is eventless, sombre even, far from spectacular. I listen to fellow commuters confuse current affairs; watch them chew gum, doze off: students, lonely housewives, dignified pensioners. A man, dressed in blue overalls, always nods at me. It is not long before we share a seat, handshakes, sandwiches and hugs. He is, for a seventy-year-old, reasonably athletic, handsome. We talk about automobiles, American presidents (Did Truman really have to drop that atom bomb? What lies in the classified Kennedy vault? What would we have done in Clinton's shoes?); graduate from carnal temptations to marital problems and confided secrets. Days fold into months – years even – and the bus-ride conversations expand into regular exchanges, conducted over pasta dishes, passion fruit and lemonade.

Gabriel Sanchez's tale (for that is my friend's name) begins in Cuba. Third in the line of thirteen siblings, he is the only journalist in an otherwise musical family. Many maestros, he says, countless musicians, from street-corner nobodies to musical saints of the Buena Vista Social Club, learnt their skills at his father's feet.

That was when Gabriel wrote articles, cutting opinion pieces for the *Cuban Times*, illuminating the Kennedy-Kruschev stalemate, often working through the night. A migraine prematurely ended one of his midnight liaisons with his typewriter.

The migraine led him home – to discover Rafael Lopez, a saxophonist for Cuba Burning (a popular but average quartet) picking pleasure fruit in his vineyard. Rosaline, Gabriel's wayward wife, gasped in horror as Gabriel Sanchez choked Rafael Lopez until he lay still, turned purple. Death by strangulation. In the nude. Rosaline died a few months later on an operating table in Havana, from a mixture of guilt and shame (medically polished as a diabetic stroke). She is said to have, even on her deathbed, scolded Rafael Lopez's ghost; a ghost rumoured to have broken typewriters at the *Cuban Times* newsroom, woken her at the crack of dawn with forlorn saxophone ballads.

And so it was that Gabriel Sanchez added murder to the family musical heritage. The glint in his eyes, his ready, guttural laughter mask a blot in his past: a migraine that exposed a worm that infested a twenty-year marriage (until then widely considered to be beyond earthly lapses). Devastated by the disappointment, on the run, he packed his bags and fled to South Africa, thousands of miles from Cuba, armed with the Spanish language and a broken heart.

Faced with evaporating finances, Gabriel turned to his dormant passion: motor mechanics. He established the Sanchez Connexion, a motor-repair workshop in

Brixton, a factory-cum-residential area inhabited by a peculiar business community: fertilizer manufacturers, coffin makers, defunct abattoirs. Gabriel is drawn to broken things, feels an urge to fix them, pull them apart, get his mind around how they work ... why they suddenly refuse to work. Apart from the many automobiles awaiting attention, the Sanchez Connexion is also full of all manner of other broken things: refrigerators, transistor radios, wrist watches and lawnmowers. It is amid broken things that I catch a fleeting glimpse of Mercedes, Gabriel's daughter. Radiant. Curious. Most humble.

7

The Newtown Cultural Precinct is nestled below the M1 South Highway. Bree Street links the precinct to Brixton and its surrounds and cuts through congested taxi ranks and swarming city traffic to the east. The Market Theatre, museums and outdoor markets are popular with arty types. A bus depot, now known to all as The Hugh, has been converted into a music academy for unemployed youth. What remains of the depot is a defunct diesel pump and three rusty double-decker buses, converted into fast-food shops. The buses are used as graffiti walls – anything from Timon and Pumba cartoon drawings to weighty reflections declaring:

FUCK THE REVOLUTION. WE CAN'T EAT HISTORY.

I, to mend my soul, steal time from the tourism booth to visit Mercedes at The Hugh – the Hugh Masekela Music Academy, where she teaches trumpet. She speaks of 'embouchure', a word of poetic ambitions: lip positioning and firmness on the trumpet mouthpiece. The students have problems with breathing, holding and sustaining long notes, marrying set musical notes with improvisation. It is admirable how Mercedes listens to rehearsal tapes and knows which particular student fails to grasp what musical tips, and which is destined for greater heights in the realm of brass instrument maestros. She knows them and guides them by instinct ... their mistakes ... their heart-warming discoveries.

I dine at a window table and listen to student practice sessions at the academy's cafeteria. The view is of a light drizzle, of Johannesburg's capitalists chasing the remains of the day: people speaking into cellphones; courier motorbikes chasing delivery deadlines; pricy automobiles emerging from underground parking into gridlocked peak-hour traffic. Things have been done to The Hugh: renovations, extensions, new paint shades. But most notable of all is the oval stage that hosts bland comedies and atrocious renditions of Shakespearean tragedies. These are on Monday and Wednesday nights. Mercedes tells me that Thursdays are the most interesting, with early evenings awarded to MC rappers spitting gut-wrenching insults, furiously waving their hands in the air, their over-size trousers hovering around their knees. The Rhyme and Reason sessions pull in a mixture of youthful and middle-aged patrons, who see nothing wrong in being commanded: 'Throw your motherfucking hands in the air. Now say Oh Oh, say O!', whereupon the performance hall blossoms with hands caught in a trance of stage lights, swaying like grass in a storm. I, upon Mercedes's insistence, catch Quiet Storm, a jazz quartet from her class. While I wait, I thaw my soul with Russian and Latin American poets on sale at the second-hand bookshop on the second floor, competing with anything from Masai bead embroidery to Yoruba masks and sculptures. The view from The Hugh window is of a street suddenly swelling with the early evening crowd, attending to cellphones, exchanging hugs; one individual displaying admirable skills with a Michael Jackson moonwalk, to cheers from smitten young things, barely dressed. There is laughter, a youthful buzz, before the street clears. I leave my poets in the company of *Guitar Lessons* and *Tennis for Beginners*, and make my way to the ticket office. I speak into the intercom, behind which is a young girl chewing gum, with earrings the size of rear tractor wheels. A thick glass separates us.

'Quiet Storm. Front row, centre,' I say.

'Cash or credit card?'

'Cash.'

I pay; the ticket is printed and slid under the glass.

'Show starts at 9:15 sharp. No smoking. Enjoy the show.'

Nine-fifteen comes, and final lighting changes and instrument tuning stops behind the curtain. I join Mercedes, on seat F16. A violin wails from behind the curtain, followed by a double-bass player running his fingers along the strings with practised skill; the way boys' fingers locate eternity between the legs of women – and women do the same between the legs of men.

The rhythm section kicks in, the curtain slowly rising to reveal spectacular lighting. A trumpeter, who we cannot see yet, ignites another standing ovation with a note so long I fear his collapse from suffocation. The spotlight follows the trumpeter from behind a gauzy screen. My mouth dries, as the trumpeter torches our collective souls with an up-tempo melody, before blasting us with a combination of high and moderate notes, all the while goading the rhythm section to such a frenzy that I worry the band will burst into flames. The trumpeter, now bending low as if trying to kiss his own knees, sends shockwaves through the venue. The crowd erupts into another standing ovation – not without good reason. Quiet Storm is like travelling to the sun.

I sit. Weeping. Perspiring. The duration of the performance is marked by the eerie silence of patrons barely moving, only the stage lights tossing and turning. I sob, dry my cheeks in guarded embarrassment. The show ends at midnight. Mercedes says: 'Tell me you are not touched, poet of mine.'

'That was something.'

'You liked it?' asks she, curious.

'Yes. It was intense.'

'Well, good. That is Spike for you. Very talented.'

'What is the name of that opening piece?' I ask. Mercedes: 'Oh, that: "Thoughts of Eternity".'

Outside, at the parking lot, the band squeezes into their faded orange Volkswagen Beetle, spewing smoke, at the mercy of rust. All that dense, textured, billowing carbon monoxide. A perfect tool to commit suicide with. I catch a glimpse of Spike: young, calm and dangerously gifted.

I, to nurture a charged affair, press a bell at 803 Jubilee Road, where Mercedes Sanchez rents an abode in one of Houghton's sought-after period apartments. Katie Melua and her 'Nine Million Bicycles' compete with a vacuum cleaner, a telephone conversation, and a whistling kettle, promising tea prospects. The vacuum cleaner retires, followed by sounds of tap water slowing then dripping to a halt. An eyeball inspects me from behind the kitchen curtain. The door opens, cautiously at first, then as if blasted by a gale-force wind. 'My poet!' says Mercedes, clutching her heart. Her embrace is firm yet gentle. Those beautiful hands, the radiant eyes. She wears a brown dress with cream polka dots, walks barefoot. Her playful smile warms the dimly lit living room, overflowing with books: famous composers competing for space with porcelain dolphins and Sean Penn films. I watch her stride to the bathroom, undress, ease herself into the bathtub. I wait. Twenty minutes. I cannot resist. I walk in, fish her leg from below the foamy water. She reads the look in my eyes, the gaze of need, pulls down a towel, dries herself with purpose while I wait in her bed. Mercedes slides in beside me, the bedside lamp catching the glow of her moist cheeks like jet fuel.

She, without warning, asks: 'When is love a burden? How can we tell if its qualities are pure, not contaminated?' She slides her hand under the sheets. It journeys from my ribs onto my chest, before u-turning and gliding down past my belly button. Meandering cautiously, it locates my rod of creation, swollen with gentle fury, ablaze with myriad sensations – enough to brighten the stars. Mercedes is good with her hands; she is the closest thing to travelling light, in the way it demands and directs attention.

'You can melt railway lines with those hands of yours,' I say. Mercedes looks unsettled and blushes at the generous, but deserved, compliment. We make love to the sound of polished masters: Wynton Marsalis; Dizzy Gillespie; Hugh Masekela. The key to sex, says Mercedes, is music: rhythm, breathing, unpredictable melodies. We rarely succumb to orchestral arrangements and when we do, I am reborn countless times over by the subtle purity of her nocturnal gasps, as pleasure drowns speech and time. I slowly let go – of the guilt that Mercedes has done nothing to deserve incomplete love, for leading her to a vineyard of love, yet refusing her full entry. Why must she suffer for Desiree's indiscretions, her stone heart?

I gaze at Mercedes's beautiful ears, her lovely neck, her maple-leaf birthmark. 'You would have made a perfect Canadian,' I tease her. Her perfection fills me with fleeting shivers, leaving me thirsty and floating. I grace her neck with hot, uneven breaths, nibble her earlobes with relentless passion. I blow air into her navel, her armpits, chew the backs of her knees, feel her spine catch fire. I disrobe her, watch her burn and curl as my quivering palm walks the Road to Damascus, to her fruit of existence. We make love again. A giggly beauty with sensual neck and deep-throated pleasure yelps. She mocks me: 'There should be a difference between loving and declaring war.' 'I know,' I say, 'but this, my tulip, is paradise, a drink from your well of fire.' Mercedes dozes off, her face aglow with passion. I, when with Mercedes, this radiant being, feel all of life's brutal scars fade and that volcanic love (last felt when washing high-school windows) return; like rain-drop patterns in swimming pools. Sustained. Effortless. Beautiful.

Mercedes saw my tears at The Hugh student performance. Her knowledge of and exposure to many types of music drives her to explain to me that part of musical mastery is learning by repetition; technique, perfecting and later breaking set rules. It pains her, she says, that I have such easy tears, that I am so deeply moved by trumpet solos (which, these days, means all the time). My tears, says Mercedes, are not to be taken lightly – for anyone who is so affected by art is a priceless gift to the universe. Money pays for music tuition fees, practice instruments, study material – but not all the mineral riches in the world will buy a single tear, shed when a fusion of instincts overwhelms the senses, ending in unexplainable sobs. This evidence of my hidden talents, she says, is what music teachers

chase all their lives – that one student who is beyond
musical scales, the one who plays hard to contain
raging fires within, who sometimes has to walk off
stage to shed a few tears.

'Easy tears, the involuntary knotting of the throat,
that gasp for breath in response to music, is a treasure,
my poet, and no amount of rehearsal ever lifts you to
that feeling of light-hearted intensity, to that trance of
sweaty palms. What, in God's universe, are you, with
such a gift, doing wasting your life on tourism sites, on
stained hospital sheets?'

8

Osama bin Laden (well, his comrades) flies aeroplanes into the Twin Towers, filling newspapers with images of devastation. Osama: a soft-spoken, bearded, skinny man with bedroom eyes. When does he dream up such destruction? Before him was Oklahoma, that Timothy what's-his-name. Yes, him. McVeigh. An American.

I watch the 9/11 anniversary with Mercedes at my side, the night of my birthday. Desiree forgets my birthday, like many others in recent times. Mercedes corrects the omission with a brand-new Dizzie Gillespie trumpet, complete with twelve red roses and a trip to Cape Town, where she is on her way for a music workshop. We fly over Johannesburg, towards a gold-plated horizon beckoning in the distance. Below is a view of clouds in many shapes and sizes: impressions of unkempt hair; dolphins without tails; some like congregants of numerous churches, floating in soapsuds. Far below are desolate farm houses, muddy swamps, meandering rivers and rocky mountain ranges. Then the coastline, with its busy highways and, finally, the airport, with its flashing lights and thundering aircraft.

The days that follow are tender escapes. Mercedes, the trumpet and I take midnight walks. There are,

with Mercedes, no beginner courtesies; she shares the
technique, weeds out the mistakes, encourages long
rehearsals. Back in Johannesburg, before we left, she
had fished an LP from her elaborate music archives
and said: 'Basics. Learn the melody on number 6.
Don't worry too much about the little lapses. Focus
on clean, round, textured notes.' In Cape Town,
Mercedes's beach obsession is Rafael Méndez. From
Miles I learn lyrical play, from Hugh intensity, from
Méndez improvisation. Mercedes gently discourages
my request to play with Quiet Storm: impatience is
the ruin of many promising musicians, she warns.
So: I blow 'A Night in Tunisia' with relish, a sense
of obsessive commitment. I suddenly realise I don't
have to think about the notes when I point my
horn skywards, I am possessed by the dictates of its
unpredictable sensations. I mourn my Desiree (not
dead but unloving); fill the trumpet with my every
possible emotion, hoping for meaning to suddenly
emerge. It never comes.

Mercedes says true trumpet mastery is about getting
lost. She listens to me practise, watches me wrestle
with my trumpet, seduce it to mirror my soul. I take
the trumpet everywhere, including on my solitary
midnight walks to the beach. I lie on my back, let the
ocean waves rinse my sandy soles, wet me up to my
armpits. I whisper to the stars, become one with the
raspy rumbles of the sea.

When I was thirteen, toiling under the Sophiatown sun, I, between pulling weeds from flower gardens, dreamt of becoming an astronaut. I still, as I did then, find starry nights and moon phases enchanting. Bra Todd nicknamed me Galileo – who owned no telescope, but a pondering heart. When a full moon bathed Sophiatown in silver light, blanketing it under heavenly calm, I composed poetry and authored those inspired letters to Desiree – letters with imagined worlds lit by a trillion moons.

The trumpet rests on my chest, glittering under the moon and purple beach lighting. I doze, succumb to foamy slumber, let the sea salt embalm my living corpse, wracked by Desiree's soullessness. A separation. By all means. But how? How does one abandon a childhood love that snuffs your life away? It is love almost gained, but sanity lost. I shiver, hug my trumpet, listen to crabs and whales, to my soul urging me to live. To shed my skin. Like a serpent. Or wither away. Like rose petals in a stained vase. Forgotten. Unloved. Dying. I rise, admire the traces of ocean-wave foam in the moonlight, walk towards the lighthouse. All is suddenly still. I point my horn to the moon, steady my thoughts, blow. A brisk tempo that evolves into Mercedes's other pet song: 'I Talk to the Trees', played by Chet Baker. A disjointed attempt, mine, but an attempt nevertheless.

A sudden easterly blows. A figure walks towards me, indistinguishable under the moonlight. I strain my eyes, see Mercedes draw nearer, walking as if gliding on the sand. Such perfect movement, such grace. She hums ballads as she walks. We lie on the beach. My head rests on her tummy, rumbling with orange juice. It is not orange juice, she says, but the mysteries of life. Like the stars we have come here to see; cosmic fires, burning thousands of millions of kilometres away. Planets. Meteors. 'Like us,' say I, 'do solar systems have wars? Moments of untold tranquillity and blinding confusion? I wonder,' I say, 'if love exists in yonder planets, where it would take zillions of lifetimes to reach. Where musical notes are blasting explosions and barbarous cosmic winds rearranging the universe.'

'Yes, my poet. But come back to earth. The sun does not know there is a Desiree wrenching your soul whenever she pleases.' We laugh. 'And further more,' she continues, 'I don't think scientists know what they are talking about.'

'They have an idea,' I say.

'Really? I beg to differ. Just how many hidden planets are there, that have direct bearing on what we know? Do stars have cousins, funeral processions? Do they lust after other stars? It is not enough to say stars die; we have to know other things. Their secrets. Obsessions. Sorrows.'

We keep still, listen to the waves battering rocks in the distance. 'That is the Milky Way, above that flashing aeroplane.'

'Yes, my tulip, it is. God spilt his milk powder.'

Laughter. A beat.

'You are the loneliest creature in the entire world, the loneliest creature I know. Let's make a baby,' she says calmly.

'Yes. Three. We'll give them Hispanic names: Conchita, Elvira, Carlos Fuentes.'

We giggle, chuckle, burst into laughter. Laughter in tune with a swelling sea, a cricket serenading night, our sighs as I cup her pulsating breasts, attempt to swallow them whole. We talk for what seems like eternity. Cuddle. Keep still. Make love under the stars, about whose secrets and sorrows we haven't the faintest clue.

Life with Mercedes is an infinite horizon of discovery: poetry readings, trumpet rehearsals. My Mercedes not only believes in, but lives for love. She knows how to measure the heart's cravings, offer embraces that leave me giddy; like a newborn baby with a fragile, rubbery neck, indifferent to the horrors of the universe. I, in her company, feel bliss without form or limits; evenings of rowdy laughter and delicate whispers. It is as if her entire life is one seamless trumpet note, graceful, arousing deep-set feelings. Gabriel Sanchez's radiant daughter, a musical charmer with a touch of erotic magic.

We refrain from romantic showmanship when Gabriel is around, she out of respect, I from a fusion of mild embarrassment and gratitude. This man, who had to murder Rafael Lopez, abandon the country of his birth, to bring me closer to the fluttering beauty of love. I owe him some measure of decency. For though he is fully aware of our molten hearts, Gabriel Sanchez says nothing, merely nods his approval. There are minor slippages, unintentional blunders, to which Mr Sanchez turns a blind eye. He knows the story of my life, can tell it as well as I. His approval (body language) is not granted in haste, and not out of ignorance. He knows Mercedes is in good hands. But the heart is a funny creature, with memories, demands of its own. I am gnawed by guilt, recalling entombed murmurs, that brutal rebuke: 'What do I have to do for you to leave me alone?'

With the University of Cape Town music workshop finished, the weekend away is over. I know: sorrow awaits me in Johannesburg.

An evening at The Hugh. Gabriel Sanchez is the only man who continues to make me laugh, share sea-deep secrets. He is the only soul who finishes my thoughts, who knows how to blunt my pain, offer measured advice, gentle encouragement. He knows about me and Mercedes but in his own generous way avoids public displays of his thoughts, wishes, objections. I am, to him, a son brutalised by life, who finds solace in the folds of his daughter's heart. One needs only to see Gabriel and Mercedes together to understand the scale of his adoration of her, to imagine how difficult it would be for him to trust anyone with the happiness of his 'Summer Breeze'.

I see him battle his thoughts; a parent's instinct to offer advice, point out life's bitter lessons. He mostly retreats to the loneliness of the Sanchez Connexion, urges us to live, explore life and its varied puzzles. About Desiree, Gabriel does offer advice. Firm advice, cushioned by peripheral jokes, and by him refilling my teacup once in a while. Love, says Gabriel, is feeling in motion. It changes character, is full of dangerously deep swamps. It attracts all of life's other feelings into a brutal cocktail of bliss beyond measure, suffering without limits. Desiree, he says, understands this; and it is up to me how much I am truly willing to lose, to do without. Obsession, the jealous little cousin of love, thrives on suffering, and has, over the centuries, mastered ways to masquerade as love. It is possible, he says, that Desiree is sincere in not believing in love – for it is not unusual for people to hold flammable opinions. It is how we respond to such opinions that sets our life's routes; the measure of suffering we are willing to endure. It is not true that love shouldn't hurt, he adds. It is too powerful an emotion to be comparable to a fleeting sneeze.

'Love is greater than life; it feeds life, makes life worth living. Why do you think we mourn the dead, erect tombstones, are willing to lay down our very lives for those we love? But be careful, young man. Love can easily be a slave to beauty. She is quite a flame, your Desiree. She probably knows it. Beautiful women

71

do know, sense these things. Men tell them all the time, so often that some of them take life, people, for granted. On the other hand, there may be things you are doing wrong. Do some soul-searching. Find out what they are. Fix them. I killed a man. For love. But was it for love? If Rafael was alive, would I be happy, knowing what I now know?' He pours me more tea, slides a saucer with his uneaten biscuit towards me. 'In your heart,' he concludes, 'lie most of the answers. Others you will find as you go along. Some warning: it will hurt. It won't make sense. You will have doubts. Be embittered. Cynical. Depressed. But love is not for the fainthearted – the most gifted of the world's charmers have suffered untold humiliations, catastrophic heartbreak. Who says love has to follow known and accepted formulas for it to be love? Poets have endured torments reducing these things to rhyming verse.'

Then Gabriel, without warning, his face fatigued, asks: 'What are you doing with my daughter?' I am about to answer but he hushes me, pours me more tea, says: 'All I am saying is, be aware what you two are up to. Life is too short for wrong steps.' It must be that I wore my heart on my sleeve, for Gabriel, who is fond of me, adds: 'Mercedes is all I have. Make your intentions clear.'

I go home numbed of all feeling, my belly bloated with tea.

9

Mercedes and I enjoy a curious ritual. We read each other's letters, answer each other's telephone calls. Not that anyone ever calls or writes to me. There are no known secrets between the two of us. A letter arrives from New York. It must be that Mercedes recognises the handwriting, the clumsy capital letters. I, upon her request, tear the envelope open, choke at the salutation: 'My May Flower Mercedes.' I stumble over sentence after sentence, thought after thought, as Benito, now a struggling actor with Broadway illusions, living on bananas and coupons, spills his entrails. The letter rambles on, with its hints of once-fiery moments with Mercedes, its attempts to recapture the magic of times past. The letter was felt in Cuba, thought in Central Park, drafted on subway trains and cabs en route to hopeless auditions, posted at a Wall Street post office.

Aside from the atrocious poetic fumbling, the puzzling baring of the soul, Benito's plight is unmistakable. He wants his May Flower back. A shiver runs down my spine, my heartbeat is unsteady. 'Not all the divine women in the world, molten and moulded into one, will compare to a single hair thread on your head.' He ends the letter with a return address. A single hair thread on your head. What was Benito smoking, to churn out such illogical images? Worse, why did Mercedes not warn me that there is a starving actor, convinced he was born to 'reinvent' Othello ('because people don't get Shakespeare'), lurking in the shadows? I have a devastating wish: that Benito be run over by a million yellow cabs, never to 'live in the ambience of your soul'.

Mercedes smiles: 'Benito – still insane as ever.'

I am agitated: 'Why keep Benito a secret from me?'

'Because. He is the past.'

'Where does he get your address then?'

'His father is friends with Dad.'

'And?'

'Family dinners, church; then one day we held hands. We were kids, maybe thirteen. Now the difficult questions: yes, he deflowered me at eighteen, and no, I don't have feelings for him anymore.'

'Why?'

'Benito does not exist in the real world. He is kind but delusional. He also has no appreciation for music.'

I fold the letter, hand it to Mercedes. She is calm, searches my eyes for signs of displeasure. She finds them: barbed wires of disappointment. My mind grinds to a furious halt. Mercedes rubs my back gently, says: 'Benito is not fit to sneeze in your presence, my poet. Steady your thoughts. The universe awaits us.'

She reaches for my forehead, plants kisses. I smell coffee on her breath.

'Good night, my poet.'

I nod.

But there is a problem. Benito does not end his love expedition with a single letter but jams the post box with an assortment of confessions and hallucinations – in rambling romantic verse, accompanied by suggestive gifts. It rains letters – mirrors of a mind under siege; a bloodhound on a love trail.

Judging by the frequency of the gifts, the cards, the nine-page poems, I can see why Mercedes declared Benito to be delusional. But there is something else: evidence of obsessive tendencies, traces of a fragile heart easily broken. The lack of response from Mercedes only sets Benito's soul on fire; spurs him to experiment with sending bits of his clothes and eyebrows in purple envelopes. A daring prophesy stands out: 'I sense I will one day disembowel myself for you.' Which, says Mercedes, is quite possible, given Benito's unpredictable excesses.

I dismiss Benito as a raving lunatic, advise Mercedes

to burn the letters on receipt. She doesn't. Her refusal, her reluctance, to free herself from Benito's insanity, his obsession with melodrama, casts a shadow on our passion. I want something else: not only for Benito to be run over by a million yellow cabs, but to be thrown down a volcano, immersed in molten lava and turned to stone. Crude. The stuff for geologists. But useless people are also the luckiest in the universe – not only do they live long, but existence seems to pander to their every whim. I brace myself to be buried in Benito's love letters, his eyebrows. Of my discomforts, I say little. The brutality of Benito's letters is in seeing Mercedes fidget with drawers, being drawn to Benito's mad chants, her gnawing preoccupation disrupting our trumpet rehearsals. To hell with Benito, I think. If he has such an excess of energy, overflowing passion, let him donate a pound of flesh, chase Desdemonas in Central Park, prove he was indeed born to 'illuminate Shakespeare'.

Insane Benito: 'I enclose my eyebrows, my floral shirt and my scent.' We, to avoid drowning in this love-Mussolini's madness, which we pity within limits, rehearse long hours. Mercedes does not compliment my haunting solos, but I, from the corner of my eye, see her eyes water. Her tears, the way she averts her head in modest and guarded embarrassment, fills me with such profound breath, such sensual light-headedness, as to blow a dozen trumpets.

I play 'I Talk to the Trees' in the mornings, 'Johannes-burg' at midday, and 'Woza Mntwana' after midnight. Chet Baker. Hugh Masekela. Abdullah Ibrahim. But

all is not well. There are times when Benito's insanity
lurks around us, polluting our thoughts, loosening
our embraces, cornering us into silences. My silences
are not completely without purpose. I know Gabriel
has profound expectations of me: 'What are you
doing with my daughter?' I, a few months ago, knew
the answer – knew, without the slightest doubt, that
Mercedes was my sun, without whose rays I would
wither and die. But somewhere between the sun's rays,
their blinding mystery, Benito's madness hid, fuelled
by fierce delusions. How do I ignore Benito, who sees
nothing wrong in committing his eyebrows through
the American postal services – onto jumbo jets, over
snow-capped mountains and oceans? It can only be
madness, the way Benito is so reckless with his love.
Our silences confirm one thing: Benito is worse than
mad. He needs not love, he needs God.

Things have changed. A choking irony stands out:
Zacharia, a former fellow prisoner, a radical poet, now
heads the Ministry of Tourism – and is, by implication,
'The Big Chief'. He offers me numerous plush jobs,
'to advance our revolution'. My answer is always the
same: 'I don't want to be important.' This offends him
greatly – for he realises that his power, to make things
happen, has unforeseen limitations. I ensure that I plan
my flu and tummy bugs well in advance, to avoid the
pompous ceremonies when he visits, quoting visitor
statistics, grinning at photographers.

Life at the Tourism Information Centre continues to be uninspiring. I, during lunch breaks, take solace in my horn. Apart from directing visitors to cemeteries and zoos, I am expected to keep records of the most visited and popular sites: cultural villages, museums, dining spots. I wonder: is there value to be found in bleak things, in a world devoid of beauty for all but the chosen few? I live in my head, in a reality that rewards club deejays more than it does midwives and neurological surgeons; a Johannesburg where suffering has no meaning.

I have, in all my days under the sun, never seen a neck as beautiful as Mercedes's – fragile yet firm; an accomplished neck, of generous warmth and minute twitches. I cannot tell which love, which beauty, is greater: Mercedes or Desiree. Desiree does not believe in love, which renders any measurement of feeling impossible. I am, when with Mercedes, incapable of any other emotion than gushes of tenderness, ticklish sensations that prompt giddy feelings beyond measure. 'What are you doing with my daughter?' asks Gabriel Sanchez. I have no answer for him, for I naturally expected such profound bliss to come from Qunu, from the rolling hills of the Eastern Cape – those Xhosa gazelles with clay-dotted faces and resolves of steel. I expected that Desiree, bred in Sophiatown, with roots in Port Elizabeth, would yield to my forlorn whispers of passion. But Cuba? I could never have anticipated, never imagined that murder would, like an ocean wave, grant me a love so great as to almost cure my mad heart. I am haunted by Benito's convictions – his refusal to give in, to accept that Mercedes and her glorious neck are beyond him.

What is Gabriel Sanchez asking, exactly? What answer is he seeking to ensure he sleeps, come nightfall? If Gabriel nudges me to make my intentions clear, given the fact that Mercedes is all he has, how much room is there for mistakes, for disappointments? Does Gabriel know that we live through a hailstorm of Benito's letters, his raging heart, his eulogies? Gabriel's question cannot be answered, for intentions point to the future, so hopelessly anchored in rusting and rotting docks of memory. I see in Mercedes's eyes the memories of holding Benito's hand that led to other, less discreet, things. How do I tell Gabriel: I have never seen so many letters, so many poems in my life; that though I find the desperation distasteful, a grain of me admires such unwavering baring of the soul without heed for audience or reward?

Even he, Gabriel, did not succeed in protecting his marriage by killing Rafael Lopez, for it is the memory of incidents past that clouds his expectations, his desires from life. Is Gabriel, in a way, saying 'disappoint me, but not too much'? But how much disappointment is forgivable – given that love of his daughter is not without puzzles? If love were to be put in a pond filled with clean water, how would it look? Would it dissolve into nothingness, or gently cruise around, like a loved goldfish? At the moment of shaving his eyebrows, stuffing them into envelopes, how does Benito's love look? Is it a goldfish, battling to find freedom from a fisherman's hook?

Is the hook of life, of dead ends, the force behind Benito's shredding of his wardrobe, his prophesying to disembowel himself if his pleadings are not heeded? A question remains: Benito and I are not the first to suffer for love, so why do we torture our hearts so? What is Gabriel Sanchez asking me, precisely? If a man walks to a public square in the nude, he is condemned as insane; yet the same man, captured on oil canvas, blurred and in unnatural colours, a bad shadow of himself, is hailed by art scholars and newshounds, in lit galleries over cheese and wine, as giving meaning to life. How am I not giving meaning to life with my love for his daughter, that Gabriel Sanchez feels entitled to interrogate me, to caution me to 'make my intentions clear'? What will Gabriel make of Benito's letters, the envelopes with eyebrows, the rosary beads dating back to many Cuban Catholic Masses?

Gabriel Sanchez visits me at the Tourism Information Centre, says Mercedes is feverish. We sit in silence, nodding into oblivion. He plays with his beard. I sense torrents of thoughts wrestling in his aged head, pulling his mind to multiple dead-ends. His brow is furrowed, his eyes narrowed, as if in an effort to arrest some thread of logic. To set his spirit free. He stirs, speaks:

'I don't have much life left in my bones. I am terrified we will let each other down.'

'How so?'

'My daughter. How great is your commitment to her?'

I don't answer but smile reassuringly.

'My intentions, Gabriel Sanchez, are to clothe your daughter in poetry for as long as we breathe. To count and name every hair on her head. To be a master of the trumpet under her tutelage.'

'And?'

'My love for Desiree cannot be wished away. I have to live with it, receive your blessings knowing you know and approve of my decades-long predicament. Desiree is undeserving, I know, but I have never known greater bewilderment.'

Gabriel Sanchez sobs briefly and intensely, stands up to leave. Just then, my cellphone rings. The husky voice is unmistakable: Mercedes of the maple-leaf birthmark.

'Hi. Please bring me some oranges and something for a sore throat, poet of mine.'

'Will do. Has Mussolini written?'

'He has utterly lost it now. The post box is totally jammed.'

'Have you thought of writing back?'

'No, my poet, I haven't.'

'Maybe you should.'

'Completely push him over the cliff?'

'The man was conceived hanging over a cliff. What is a little nudge between friends?'

We laugh. But it is not funny, in the moral sense.

10

It is early afternoon. My contract with the Tourism Information Centre ends today. I return home to find Mercedes asleep. The key under the door carpet lets me in, and a glance at her teaching schedule on the refrigerator confirms she missed a trumpet improvisation class. I place the oranges on the dining table, decide against waking her; sip left-over wine from a bottle and ease myself onto a recliner chair in her library. My focus settles on book spines, ranging from studies on Vivaldi and the Four Seasons, to African Traditional Instruments, to Modern Orchestral Conductors. I, as is the Mercedes tradition, light a scented candle next to her porcelain dolphins – and the library is bathed in vanilla scents. My thoughts are scattered, my mood edgy. The wine warms the belly, fools the brain into temporary bliss, leaving nerve ends aroused and twitching.

Something unexpected happens. I watch a moth, proud of its brown and deep-orange wings, circle the candle, drawn to the beauty of the flame. The love affair is at first full of caution, before becoming increasingly daring, reckless even; then, disaster. In an instant, quicker than fate, the moth wing dips into the candle wax – ending the moth's playful flight in smoky cremation. I watch as the flame consumes the insect, leaving a helpless head dripping with crystallising wax. The scene is very reminiscent of Desiree and I – with Desiree the confident flame, and I the suicidal moth.

With the wine bottle for company, shielding me from my over-cautious nature, I think: what in the nature of some insects attracts them to light, to fiery ends? Surely, the red wine suggests, there should be more important things in life than why moths continue to be humiliated by candle flames? It should be possible to admire flames from afar. But I cannot deny that the true nature of flames is that they offer warmth; an even truer measure is the fact that they burn. My companion, the wine, takes effect, blurring life's conundrums into tolerable irritants. Mercedes is fast asleep, her breathing peaceful. I place the oranges next to her, together with the pills for a sore throat, and walk to the bridge. To think. All of three hours.

I return home to find Mercedes watching Larry King in the library – not really watching, but sobbing. Long, drawn-out, quivering body sobs, with both her palms wiping away tears that refuse to dry up. Those beautiful hands, mopping up the tears, as if they were windscreen wipers. My attempts to rub her shoulders, her arched back, only intensify her weeping, which has left her perfect eyes bloodshot and swollen. I have never seen her so overwhelmed, inconsolable. She takes an eternity to calm down, to say, almost

inaudibly: 'Dad wants us to return to Cuba.' Gabriel
Sanchez, failing to get satisfactory answers from me,
has decided to hang me by the testicles in a public
square. Knowing me as he does, he has dismissed
me as a failure: a mildly accomplished journalist,
a hesitant revolutionary, a looming failure at the
institutions of poetry and marriage, parrot of tourism
information, laundryman checking hospital sheets
for stains, promising trumpeter, futile philosopher
thinking in circles about love and life without reaching
any conclusive opinions.

'When?' I ask her.

'In a week.'

'But why?'

'Dad prefers dying on Cuban soil. That has always
been his covenant with the family.'

'What is wrong with South African soil? I thought he
liked it here.'

'So did I. You could come with us to Cuba.'

'I don't want to be buried on a tropical island.'

There is a long silence, a silence of wounded thoughts.
What are you doing with my daughter? People. One
never truly knows with them. One moment Gabriel
is volunteering pearls of wisdom on what makes
life complete, the next he prefers to die on Cuban
soil. What do I know about Cuba, except bits and

pieces gathered from conversations with Mercedes? The little that everyone else seems to know: Cigars. Castro. Che. Not much else. In truth, the greatest blow is in acknowledging that I am no different from any other moth; that some candle flames follow you. Two betrayals in one: the first from a reluctant father-in-law masquerading as a friend; the second from a passionate would-be wife with daughter obligations, a void to fill for a wayward mother and her Rafael Lopez misdemeanours. How could I possibly abandon Johannesburg? How is love of Mercedes greater than love of home? The South Africa in an Africa stirring with hope and abundant possibilities; an Africa that is a moth refusing to burn.

A week. Imagine.

A windy morning. I visit Gabriel Sanchez at the workshop. The For Sale sign is replaced by telephone numbers of the new owners, Jaco & Seun. There are three cars standing in line, washed and awaiting collection. A Ford Custom. A Toyota hearse. A bright red Chevrolet El Camino with a flat front tyre. Discarded parts are heaped on a tractor trailer, the workshop itself clean and empty, except for a refrigerator with a missing door.

Gabriel is busy with a lawnmower, a rusty orange thing with oil leaks and blunt blades. Something has snapped between us. His body language has changed. He takes too much time sorting and selecting his tools, folding and packing oily rags, as if I am invisible. He normally requests a hand with moving heavy engine blocks or holding the torch to detect leaks; but not today. He seems brutally relaxed for someone with a trip to Cuba pending, uprooting many years of existence in a foreign country. His lunch box is untouched, his eyes dart with a borderline resentment. He hammers at a scrap lawnmower engine, robs it of its useful parts to fix the other one, until sweat drips from his forehead, from his aged and fluffy-haired scalp. I sit and wait for him to finish his lawnmower diagnosis; to collect his thoughts, or at least say something about the weather. He says nothing. I expect hostile stares from him, but when he speaks his eyes are kind, his voice gentle.

'Old age is more about fading away than making new plans. You work within your limitations, without the luxury of second chances.' Gabriel dabs a rag in petrol, wipes oil-leak grime from the lawnmower engine. He uses a small brush to clean the tight corners, to restore the ancient engine to acceptable levels of decay. The attention he pays to the minutest speck of dirt is not merely diligent work, but punishment by silence. It is punishment meant to break but not crush me, to burn yet still leave redeemable valuables; to convey deep displeasure without resorting to disdain. But I did not send Rafael Lopez to prune Sanchez's vineyard, nor did I compel Gabriel to commit murder. Yes, he is disappointed that there are no guarantees for his Summer Breeze. Understandably so. But also puzzling. Infuriating. Perplexing. Yet I seek to understand, to dismantle him bolt by bolt, make sense of his abrupt silence. Like violin strings snapped in mid performance. Eighteen years of wrestling my temperament, of thinking myself in and outside of existence, guide me to calmly state: 'I am not that important, Mr Sanchez, that you should wrack your soul so. I have accepted that you return to Cuba with your daughter. It is most admirable how you have raised her, how well she speaks of you. I wish, lastly, to say that the world has changed since Castro's Cuba. The idea of family is, in our century, but a fantasy. We are, in these times, in the business of random fucking, of maiming hearts. Even in Cuba. Mercedes is all you have, I know. But a part of her belongs to me. I pray it were possible for you to be granted a century more of life – but even that extension will some day come to an abrupt end. Then what? Absence is as important as presence – for both have the power to mould and alter things.'

He is disarmed, yet amazingly blunt: 'So, are you also in the business of random fucking?'

'No, sir.'

'Of maiming hearts, then?'

'No.'

'In your own words, you say she belongs to the universe, to this century. Isn't the randomness that you speak about the product of a century where family is a fantasy? How are we any different from a troop of monkeys then?'

Good listener, Mr Sanchez. There is in his thinking, however, a certain faulty reasoning; insanity, if you like. And no one seems to know where to find the keys to the mad house. I recall few times when I have felt this bad, this sick – as if I have drunk gallons of vinegar.

True to his word, the possessive Mr Sanchez, protective of his daughter, terrified of the plagues of old age, leaves Johannesburg. Not without his Mercedes. But Mercedes's departure is not a simple matter of flying out on South African Airways Flight 1337. It signifies not only the end to an era, some minor adjustment to be made along life avenues, but an injustice of major proportions. What more is there to say, to ask, to understand? She left. 'You are the loneliest creature I know.' Those were her words.

Three years pass. In time, I forget her.

The Moolman Laundry Services was gutted by fire yesterday. An electrical fault or some such. Black, billowing smoke and multiple destruction. Under-insured, Mr Moolman had little choice but to count his losses and let everyone go. I am behind with my rent. Ms Tobin, the agent at Renaissance Properties, is relentless with her threats of eviction.

My defence is honesty.

I don't make up stories about non-existent emergency funerals or delayed bank deposits. I tell her that not only do I not have the money, but that I also don't have a plan. As months one and two pass, Ms Tobin becomes increasingly impatient, writing a letter a week to remind me of my breach of the rental agreement. Mr Bemba, the building owner, is headed for South Africa for a week or two and 'it is only sensible to have all the paperwork and money above board'. Ms Tobin presses me to make a plan, to which I answer:

'I play the trumpet for donations.'

'So you are not a professional musician?'

'Almost, but no.'

I clear a hundred and fifty rand on a good day from passers-by to whom I have not yet become a nuisance. But good days are few and far between – so I make do with a vase full of cents for bread rather than rent for a Johannesburg suburban apartment.

Raising enough rent money would mean I would have to be on my trumpet thirty days non stop, in five different city spots at the same time – praying that the day ends with a few crumpled notes (thrown in grudgingly) and not rusty coins.

It makes sense to me why people stay in soul-denting jobs: to avoid worse humiliations – sneers and jeers from strangers armed with disdain for artistic expression. Johannesburg can be saintly, giving; but it takes a while to distinguish the carefree spendthrifts from stone-hearted stingy souls – those that rebuke me for unspecified transgressions, rather than applauding my heartfelt ballads. I live on bananas and bread, sometimes with sour milk, to save extra from my earnings. But there are unexpected consequences: the milk loosens the bowels, making trumpet-blowing a risky prospect. Another sore point: I have to put something aside for the Metro Police, whose enforcement of municipal bylaws is synonymous with free lunches and dipping into my meagre earnings.

There are also random demands by them for specific songs to be played at the drop of a hat. Talk of salt in the wound! To rob a man, and then expect him to provide the musical ambience while you feast. Like a jukebox. Tragic. I can, above the wail of the trumpet, sometimes hear someone say: 'This thing is just flesh and bones. Is he trying to commit suicide, blowing that damn trumpet?' Or The Hugh night-watchman, muttering: 'Lazy shit, he thinks money grows on trees.'

My trumpeting is marked by an eerie detachment. By my age, life expects of one to have prepared a cushioned nest for retirement, to have accepted the blunders committed during youth and be prepared for a life of increasing solitude. 'Old age is more about fading away than making new plans. You work within your limitations, without the luxury of second chances,' said Gabriel. But fate singled me out for an uncertain life, a life of futile aspirations, stillborn in a Pretoria penitentiary.

It is true that I look gaunt; a recluse, an irritation. My humiliations at the Mary Fitzgerald Square continue, as do the exasperated phone calls from Ms Tobin. Mr Bemba's trip has been postponed by a month or two. I begin to doubt if he exists at all. I sleep badly, fearing Renaissance Properties will lock me out, throw my modest belongings on the street. This year's winter is devilish, eliminating any prospect of my returning to park benches. Apart from freezing to death, I cannot afford to risk losing my trumpet to theft or mugging. The profound sentimental value aside, the trumpet is the only thing that keeps my soul intact.

In other matters my life is no less bleak. Desiree has attempted to resume contact. I finally make my decision, decades too late, to rid myself of her. I avoid her phone calls (a high-flying career woman with obscene job demands, and a rent fugitive too embarrassed to ask for food); ignore her knocking at my front door, once or twice a fortnight; her vague notes: 'I am not a plague. Call me. Desiree.'

From behind the curtain, I see her Jaguar in the driveway, the ever-adoring Amazu smiling blissfully in the passenger seat. I am afraid of Desiree, the way one fears a lightning bolt known to set fire to things.

My shock is profound when Amazu, a few weeks later, leaves a note on my door, saying: 'Urgent. Desiree in hospital.' A phone call from Rosebank Medical Centre confirms she has asked for me. What could possibly be wrong with her? Her bedside is full of her lawyer colleagues, legal minds speaking in murmurs. They applaud her diligence, her profound knowledge of the law, so persistently that it sounds like an obituary. None of them pay me much attention – probably dismissing me as one of her poor relatives; Africans and their intricate family trees, multiple relatives crawling out of the woodwork on days of trouble. None of them know anything about how well she sings, or that she never believed in love.

I immediately feel out of place, yet press on to greet them. She lies in typical hospital helplessness: big pipe in her mouth, smaller pipes in her nostrils. Twice, her heart failed. Technically speaking, she was dead for twenty seconds, but quick reflexes from the doctors ensured she was electrocuted back to life, followed by sixteen-hour surgery, to fix the clogged arteries. But there are complications. An undetected fault in the oxygen tank means Desiree is no longer Desiree as I know her. Where will I ever get answers, now that she is brain dead? All that fiery temper and tonnes of guilt, finally confirming one thing: she is human after all. But at what point did she call for me? Did she know, sense, that her brain would suffocate, succumb to accident under local anaesthetic? Was her calling for me a moment of repentance, to say she believed in love now? There is the impression of a smile playing about her lips; or maybe it is just the involuntary twitching of a body under siege.

But weren't the notes she left, the message calling me

to her bedside, in themselves acts of love? I am not a plague. Call me. Why are you running away from me? Call me: so that I can tell you of my profound discovery of love. You are now free to stare at me. Was she sensing impending loss of control, a jittery heart threatening to engulf her in eternal regrets? But would her transformation have endured, had she seen me as I now am, gaunt from a banana-and-sour-milk diet? I am certain she would not have recognised me; the destitute trumpeter chasing donations at Mary Fitzgerald Square.

With ruptured arteries, a brain never again able to ponder legal arguments, she, too, is no longer the same. Alive only because she is still breathing. The tragedy has brought a measure of certainty to my life. It will never be known why Desiree called for me during her darkest hour. My Desiree, who waited too long, miscalculating the power of her charms.

What will Amazu do? Hope for a miracle? Or will he, with his mathematical mind, give the go-ahead for the machines to be switched off? I picture him, running away from fate; clipping her still-growing toenails, reporting beeping drips, squeezing an increasingly wooden palm, kissing the parched lips never to sing 'Amazing Grace' again. Yet how can Amazu ever understand the thrill and angst of peering at Desiree from behind curtains, watching her fix Bra Todd's shirt buttons – the small, practised movements of her wrist, the slight tilt of her head to the side, the biting off of the sewing thread between her teeth, her frown declaring her thoughts to be on things beyond the attaching of shirt buttons? Or the ecstasy of hearing her sing, watching her on stage with the Fleeting Birds (how charming she looked in floral dresses, ravishing in red, hypnotic in creams). There were many singers in Sophiatown, yet none seemed to hold a melody quite like Desiree, and if they did, it always seemed to me the crude flaunting of talent rather than a God-given grace.

Amazu arrives, obscured by a big bunch of flowers; flowers which, as things stand, Desiree is incapable of acknowledging. It would not make any difference if he placed a donkey jawbone by her bedside instead. Fickle, the meanings humans attach to things. Why should a donkey jawbone, given in smitten admiration, not be equivalent to a bunch of flowers?

Amazu is red-eyed. Hurt; poor mathematician. His pronouncement sounds assured yet crazy: 'She will pull through.' The lawyer colleagues know, as I do, that she won't pull through – but still they say: 'She will. Dee is a fighter.' No one, not even Desiree, cheats confirmed brain damage. The reality is clear. Amazu must prepare for a funeral. Maybe in a month, or two, maybe in a year, or ten, depending on his appetite for hospital visits. I shake his hand, say: 'You wouldn't have something to eat on you, would you?'

There is disbelief from the lawyers, freshly stuffed from Sandton restaurants and cafeterias.

'No,' says Amazu, taken aback.

'Never mind.' I shuffle out of ward C3, hungry, drowsy. Not sad or courting rage. I am simply overwhelmed.

At the hospital entrance, I am met by a thunderstorm: hailstones, psychotic wind, flying leaves and other debris, blown too fast to be identified. Rosebank trees are combed by the tyrant wind, shooting dry twigs into the air. The downpour is unexpected and the hailstones turn the route to Verona Estates, two blocks away, into a war zone. I am too hungry to run, so I walk up Tyrwhitt Avenue, past The Grace Hotel, and turn left towards Jellicoe Avenue. The Verona Estates entrance is heaped with hailstones, the impression of an icy grave, piled with ice instead of soil. I am drenched and shivering.

I step over the grave, walk past the courtyard, around the rose garden guarded by falcons carved from stone, onto the cobalt staircase to number 144. A whimpering fox terrier sits on the doormat. There are many things in its eyes: a touch of fear, but also guarded expectation. I notice the limp in its gait, one of its back legs barely touching the floor. I feel exasperated. 'Out of the more than one hundred units,' I say to the puppy, 'you had to choose mine?' I also feel relief: Renaissance Properties have not locked me out. Yet.

I pick the puppy up, a lovable cream and brown creature. It shivers in my hand, dripping with melting hailstones. I dry my visitor with a towel, for which he licks my hand in gratitude, throw a match under the logs in the fire place, and the room is gradually enveloped by warmth. The reason for the limping is soon found: a thorn is lodged in the small paw. I construct a nest using towels and couch cushions, offer my visitor some bread soaked in sour milk. He cleans up the plate. I offer him red wine on a saucer (local anaesthetic) to blunt the pain from that thorn. Cabernet Sauvignon, left-over from days of better fortune. The puppy rolls onto its back while I tickle its underbelly. I keep refilling the saucer; watch the pink tongue whip it up. My visitor begins to doze, from warmth and unexpected hospitality. One quick pull and a drunken yelp, and the thorn is out. I show it to the puppy: 'Reason for your suffering,' and throw the thorn into the fire.

I change into dry clothes and return to find the puppy fast asleep. Drunk maybe. Bread and sour milk, multiple saucers of wine and a fire – shared with a sudden dog friend. I know I have created expectations, bound myself to be provider and protector. 'Benito. Yes. That is your name from today.' The puppy stirs, then sinks into an even deeper sleep. I continue: 'Welcome, but no barking in the house. Rent, Benito. We have rent problems here, my friend. You are lucky your thorn is out, but nothing can be done about Desiree. Anyway, good night Mussolini. Good Nederburg this, straight from the Cape winelands. I have some left-over cents, something for breakfast. I must warn you, though – ours are small Greek and Chinese shops, or Indian shops, hidden from the glare of mall opulence. We are always short of money, you see, so the smaller shops make the brutal humiliations somewhat more private.

'The reason we are broke? There are many. You see, I am an astronaut at heart, a poet. That is what I would like to be paid for. Being a poet. Not the kind that simply throws a beret on the head, with an unkempt beard, reading to five people in elite bookshops. Not the kind with predictable metaphors: chains, fire, eternity, time. Phew! We are about existence, Benito, searching for meaning where many claim to have found it – their freedom our pain, their complacency our silent rage. Are you listening, you Italian dictator? I am caught in the tragedies of love – so no barking please. I don't know how you dogs express subtlety, how you get someone's attention. Raise a paw, blink. Roll on your back. About tomorrow: you can stay home if you want but my work is at the Mary Fitzgerald Square. We play the trumpet for fools. Plans for the future? We don't even have a funeral plan, my friend. Other work? What other work? Don't you see these able-bodied young men on street corners with despair in their eyes – packed by the truckload to fill potholes, dig furrows, carry logs? They also live on bread and milk. They stink? Tell me something new. Their labour is cheap, so what do you expect they should buy? Bread or perfume? How is that paw now? Better? Good. Time for bed, my homeless friend. I miss my Mercedes. You know what she said to me? "You kiss with military precision, my poet. Your embrace is as delicate as the hands of a bomb technician." She then left me.'

11

I am woken by insistent barking. Benito has woken before me. The rain continues to pour down, in determined torrents rumoured to ignite lust and longing. There is no bread or sour milk left – and, by the look of things, no chance of trumpet donations today. But today is different from other days – there is the dog to worry about. I sleepwalk through the morning rituals. Benito follows me around from room to room, finally settling in front of the television. What do dogs make of CNN? Of world markets and strife in Zimbabwe? There is a knock at the door, decisive, bordering on rude. I open: Ms Tobin, accompanied by a young Indian couple, who push sleeping twins in a pram.

'Morning,' says Ms Tobin. 'Sajiv and Ranjeni Naidoo. New tenants, here to view the apartment.' No advance warning, no courtesy call, no appointment. In this dreadful weather. I nod, shake hands with the Naidoos. Sajiv is large and imposing, married to a small woman of mouse-like movements. 'I like it,' declares Sajiv, even before walking past the open-plan kitchen. 'Check out the wall art, Ran. I already feel at home.' I am amused. Irritated. My looming homelessness aside, what kind of man makes such erratic, impulsive decisions? Ranjeni simply nods away. I pray that she hates the place. But she doesn't. She thinks the wall paintings are exquisite.

'Madman, this Mugabe,' says Sajiv as we reach the living room. 'Check out the bookshelves, Ran. Beautiful. We will take it,' comes the death knell. Ms Tobin beams. My stomach knots. I, in the absence of coffee or juice, offer the intruders refrigerated water. Sajiv rambles on. In fifteen minutes, I learn he is the MD of a mining company; has cancelled dentist appointments to be here; lived in Prague for a time; has a twin brother who is a leading mind in microbiology. Not only that: he cannot find a temporary house good enough for the twins (Thiloshnee and Vassie), and plans ultimately to immigrate to Australia. Sajiv has an opinion about everything. Ranjeni is mildly embarrassed; yet her demeanour suggests a repressed cynic not easily impressed. Where Sajiv surges with rushed conclusions, the steely Ranjeni ferments with thoughtful considerations, open-ended commitments. These two: chalk and cheese.

Ms Tobin promises to prepare the lease for collection by close of business. She intends to have everything wound up with me by then. 'Use the banking details in the email,' she tells the Naidoos. 'Keys and gate remote will be handed over once the contract is signed.' She walks them out. Their goodbyes are drowned by an amusing tragedy: I am a homeless soul with a bookcase full of books, owner of a trumpet and a stray dog. Ms Tobin returns shortly. She tries hard to come across as remorseful, but her eyes betray her. 'I truly sympathise with your predicament. But we have limited options here,' she says. I nod. 'You can move your belongings to our storeroom in the meantime. For a fee.'

'Predicament' does not begin to describe my circumstances. There is nothing more unforgiving than Johannesburg winters. I dread the frost, the fevers, the prospect of aching bones. There is an even more sinister reality: I cannot expect Johannesburgers to stand around the city precincts in freezing weather, listening to tempestuous trumpet notes.

12

The soul is a temperamental thing. Once tainted, there is little to be done to restore its tranquillity. Like window glass smudged by oily hands, leaving erratic dirty handprints that obscure views of a complete universe. But there is an uncomfortable truth: souls are not designed to be tranquil – and if there are any such, they are so few as to render their existence meaningless. That is what I learnt in prison – a conclusion reached after many years of reflection. Yet meaning still eludes me; for the world is full of flammable opinions.

It will never make sense to me why the eighteen-year punishment. I admit: I am not a Desmond Tutu. Or a Nelson. I have come to realise that underlying my apparent indifference is irresolvable anger; anger in search of meaning. There is a risk that I will die without completely ridding myself of this terrible predicament, aging with smouldering resentment, a sense of brewing rage. But the injustice that I feel is nothing new. Che Guevara commanded guerrilla warfare while wrestling with bouts of asthma, yet he died with little reward. All those months in the woods, attacking and escaping from Batista's men, and on the grand march to Bolivia. And the reward? An execution.

Major Joubert was right in warning me that I should not be a martyr. But he was also wrong. Martyrdom is not only when you are dead and buried; there are many walking dead, bruised by the revolution. A revolution which, by the look of things, has lost its way – in the *Animal Farm* and Kafkaesque sense. How is one expected to plead justifications for one's continued existence to gun-wielding thugs – thugs that emerge out of nowhere, demanding things?

I return to sleeping on park benches. There are times when it feels like the winter will never end, when the cold nights seem to be doubling into endless spikes determined on drawing blood. There is Benito to worry about; so I wrap him in plastics, in discarded garments, anything resembling warmth. Johannesburg is one grey mortuary, cold and lonely. Frost descends on Benito and I with relish, leaving park benches and grass a silver-fish white. Other beggars? Of course there are. But they are too involved in their unknown thoughts to sustain any proper conversation. So I talk to the dog instead. What about? Well, we talk about the revolution. All I need do, I tell the dog, is speak to the comrades I know. Not many words. There is a particular language, a language of immediate responses. Comrade A speaks to Comrade G who presses Comrade Q for an answer. Who is he? Comrade Q will ask. One of us, the others will say. Not exactly in the trenches, but he risked death supporting our cause. A long imprisonment, and not one comrade betrayed.

But I cannot bring myself to say the words needed to

escape the biting winters and vagabond life; this life of torrential humiliations. I have my reasons. I have never believed in easy, predictable things. I have, in my mind, not worked out what may happen if Comrade Q indeed offers that cushy job to me. Will I be expected to owe him favours? Of what kind? Even more absurd: how many souls owe how many Comrade Qs favours?

There is yet another problem: being an accidental politician (a newspaper columnist, really) has its burdens. It is a revolution for sissies, typing rhetorical observations from the safety of a newsroom. I crossed no borders, hid in no trees or muddy swamps. Comrade Q has every right to disdain my requests, award the perks to more deserving revolutionaries. It is this uncertainty that I cannot bear, this endless weighing and counter-weighing of options, the scrutiny demanded by prospects without guarantees. Everyone serves at the pleasure of Comrade Q. And, worse, everyone wants to be Comrade Q. That is why I choose instead the certainty of Johannesburg winters, the solace of the trumpet. There is a certain freedom, a peculiar reckless abandon, that comes with not being important. Humiliations hide a secret power, of pin-point observation, of righteous anger. In other words, I am always free to tell Comrade Q, whoever he is, to fuck off. What is existence without the divine principle of free will?

Morning comes. It is with these thoughts that I see dawn sweep in over grey and lifeless skyscrapers, the first rays of the sun, summoning park birds to a melodious concert. We worship the sun, Benito and I. How else are we expected to thaw? Benito stirs, his belly pink and empty. I will have to make a plan, pawn some Wordsworth or Aristotle for bread and sour milk. Prized poets and philosophers, bought for a pittance, resold for a fortune. Second-hand bookstore keepers; fucking vampires.

Johannesburgers. In all directions they walk, speaking into cellphones, arranging their lives. From the Bree Street taxi rank music blares, to raucous laughter from taxi drivers around a fire. There is a name for this music. It's called kwasa-kwasa. Congolese. Erotic dancing. It is as if the taxi drivers have no bones, the way their waists gyrate to the spellbinding guitar arrangements, the way they touch themselves in feather-light mime. I approach, Benito following close behind, whimpering from the cold. I have only one thing in mind: the fire. Taxi drivers are known to be rough, to hold flammable opinions. The dancing stops, the laughter subsides. The fire is tempting, inviting. The ash that surrounds the steel bucket confirms this as a morning ritual; lonely taxi drivers ferrying all manner of souls to Johannesburg's cardinal points.

'Man and dog,' says a bearded one, smiling broadly. Laughter. Benito whimpers close to me, settles down next to my torn boots.

I greet.

'*Yebo*,' comes the chorused response.

'May I share your fire please, gentlemen?' I ask, my teeth clattering.

They look at me suspiciously, with repressed laughter.

'But you are already warming yourself, without the permission you seek. You and your dog,' says an irritable queue marshall. They are full of questions, judgements. I half warm myself next to their fire, field a barrage of questions. Where am I from, with a dog, so early in the morning, why do I look like I ate eleven months ago, what is in the case that hangs over my shoulder?

'A trumpet,' I answer.

'A boy scout?' comes a question from a shadow masked by wood smoke.

'A trumpeter.' They laugh. One walks to his taxi, returns with bread and avocados. 'Have something to eat,' he says. 'You will have to see about your dog.'

Benito looks at me, expecting his share of the bread. I ignore him, and his whimpering. My bones begin to ache as the warmth thaws the winter cold. I choke on bread and emotions, a deep sense of gratitude so profound that I hold the bread to my bosom, shaking. Benito continues to whimper, his eyes on the bread. 'Johannesburg dogs,' quips the bearded one. 'Since when do dogs desire bread?' There is raucous, indulgent laughter. The passenger queues grow.

'Rosebank, Sandton, Alex, Eastgate,' says the queue marshall, his mouth full of bread. 'Randfontein, Soweto, Melrose, Tembisa,' he adds, between whistles. Like roaches the taxis leave the rank, one by one, packed with pondering clientele. The fire dies down, taking with it the comfort of temporary warmth. Benito looks at me, reproachful, a touch of distrust in his eyes. I offer him bread. He sniffs. Looks the other way. Why do I have to put up with this temperamental dog? I snap my fingers at him. He ignores me. I walk towards Mary Fitzgerald Square, see Benito battle quick decisions, then reluctantly follow my heels in motion. A hungry, agitated, mistrustful dog on my tail. I feel sick.

Along Bree Street there is an impromptu roadblock; body searches, scrutiny of suspicious characters. Three youths lie belly down on the concrete, police dogs sniffing and growling. I am lined up with others against the wall, almost searched. Visible policing, they call it. I offer my name and my trade (trumpeter) and am allowed to pass without being frisked. It must be that I look harmless – an unfortunate trait to have in the unpredictable streets of Johannesburg.

Mary Fitzgerald Square is unusually deserted, except for the pigeons fluttering overhead. I adjust the trumpet case on my shoulder, continue thawing in the mid-morning sun. Someone has lost a twenty-rand note; fortuitous taxi fare, to visit Desiree. I walk back to the Bree Street taxis, stand in the Rosebank queue, the visibly hungry dog at my feet. The ride is smooth. Benito lies at my feet, unobtrusive. I suspect he will not last a week on Johannesburg streets, so there is a profound commitment in hoping I can delay his death. One never knows when life will decide to cease. The rest of the trip is eventless; along Jan Smuts Avenue, through leafy suburbs hidden behind high walls and trees. At Twelfth Avenue my trip ends, followed by a ten-minute walk to the Rosebank Medical and Dental Centre. A sign at the hospital reception warns:

NO PETS.

I leave Benito with a group of bored children who, like dogs, are not allowed in the high-care wards. I follow streams of jubilant and sombre next-of-kins along corridors to all sorts of wards, mount a flight of stairs to ward E84. The other three beds are empty. Only Amazu is there, sitting at Desiree's bedside, his eyes red from weeping. I greet him with pity and feel a sudden stir of emotions (his sobs of futile hope, his doomed protest against euthanasia). There is no doubting Amazu's grief. The matter is not complicated: Desiree is alive, but also dead. I have never been good at comforting people, so I let him sob, whispering his futile prayers. Desiree is ignorant of her suffering. Her lips are dry and peeling, her complexion artificially polished by drips, and that sharp tongue, mute. Death circles her, taking its time, torturing the living. She has not opened her eyes in weeks, says Amazu. 'It must be dreadful, hearing things you cannot respond to,' he adds. In the greater scheme of things, Desiree is not much different from the ward furniture. She has put me through living hell, at some subtle level has enjoyed seeing me tortured. So I draw a measure of perspective from this living corpse of a beauty undecided whether to live or die. There is a certain comfort in knowing Desiree will never torment me again; not in the flesh. Maybe this is what love is – accepting the crudest possible treatment with the grace of a wise monk, the selflessness of a saint. It occurs to me she is, in her fifties, at the crossroads, the place where women outgrow the arrogance of youth and embrace the unpredictability of ageing.

How do I tell her what my life has become? That I have learnt to dodge Johannesburg winters by escaping to shopping-mall restrooms, to use the hand driers against the evil chills – also to blow-dry Benito, watch his fur part to reveal pink, shivering flesh. What will she make of this blow-drying of a dog? Will it be to her an act of supreme humanity, or a waste of compassion? Desiree will never understand that my adoration of her has always had a preordained basis, that it was in the greater scheme of the universe, never just some average emotion. She will never understand the nagging heartbreak of being separated from her, the trauma of the fall of Sophiatown, and of my imprisonment. But I, in my heart, still believe that, given enough time, I had in me sufficient poetry and resolve to pursue her until she finally gave in out of raging love – or as the only logical escape from my constant pleadings. It is true that Amazu and I are both suffering, but for sentiments and ponderings of different kinds.

13

A mazu insists I lodge with him, 'until such time you are back on your feet'. Apart from possible pneumonia, he adds, it is morally unacceptable that I curl under freezing Johannesburg skies, while he has a spare room occupied by an ageing cat. 'It will be summer in another few weeks,' I tell him. 'There is no need to rob your cat of his lodgings.' Amazu murmurs something about my suicidal tendencies – tendencies confirmed by Desiree on several occasions.

I accompany Amazu to 184 Jan Smuts Avenue in Parkhurst, to the three-bedroom house he now shares with Algebra the cat. It is a chaotic house: a sink full of dirty dishes; lone shoes competing with mathematics textbooks on the floor; stained tea cups, banana peels and pizza boxes on the couches. Algebra sits on the couch between old newspapers and discarded yoghurt containers, the chaos completed by an assortment of toothbrushes, dish cloths, chicken bones and armies of ants. A thin veil of dust coats most of Amazu's belongings, at which he, mildly embarrassed, protests: 'From dust we come, to dust we shall return.'

The room I am led into is a small, sun-facing haven with roof-high windows hidden by rusting blinds.

There is little in the way of furniture, except for a creaky bed and a defeated couch. There was some attempt at interior decor: sandy wooden floors, cream walls, dusty burgundy blinds, African sculptures and cream and brown bed sheets. A cat's nest (a wooden box with a red blanket) and a wooden milk bowl are at the centre of the room – a peculiar shrine, blessed with cat fur and urine, in which Algebra engages in matters of cuisine, giving off a distinctive animal smell.

I make a special request: that Algebra the cat continues to live in his room (it is not my intention to displace anyone) as my room-mate. There is evident dislike between Algebra and Benito, with the temperamental dog often expelling the aged white cat.

Amazu's own room is only slightly more orderly than the rest of the house – as orderly as a neglected horse stable: more mathematics textbooks, fused light bulbs, stray laundry. Yet there is, despite this overwhelming chaos, little complication in Amazu's life. Eccentricities and abundant laziness maybe, but little turmoil. Conversations and host courtesies extended to me are marked by extreme humility; a mind that seems centuries ahead of our immediate surroundings. A precise mind that prepares tea as if solving for x – or determining puzzles in trigonometry. It is disarming how basic Amazu's life is, how the muted radio sounds in the kitchen preside over an existence stripped to its bare bones. Objects are searched for and located on a needs basis. I cannot fathom how he knows where to look for things: particular toothbrushes, coffee mugs, nail clippers. But he does and, more than that, he also knows where to find unsolved mathematical problems, strewn across the house.

A hopeless cook, Amazu orders French fries and marinated chicken for dinner. I nibble something to stop myself from collapsing. My thoughts are still at the hospital. How is it possible that such fiery love goes to waste? If there was ever a point to life and living, how come *homo sapiens sapiens* continues to get most things so dreadfully wrong? As if reading my thoughts, Amazu unexpectedly lets loose: Desiree always wondered aloud why I insist on doing everything the hard way, he tells me. Why I think I can wrestle the universe into submission, my lone pursuit of non-existent perfect worlds. The reason for her withholding her love, he goes on, was that she was never sure what to make of my kind of love, a love that withstood her most brutal rebukes. Yet, at the same time, she confessed an admiration for my commitment. It was this contradiction, with a dash of guilt thrown in, that complicated matters of romantic privilege.

Lousy, callous reasoning – but reasoning nevertheless.

Life is painfully predictable in Amazu's household. He catches a bus to the University of the Witwatersrand every morning. We live on take-aways. I write poetry and practise the trumpet between sleeping (more like hibernation) and our visits to the hospital. Tedious routine. I am often woken by Amazu singing in the shower, so well that it is hard to know who the real Andrea Bocelli is. I don't like opera much myself. It always sounds to me as if the singers are trapped in torture chambers, desperately bellowing for help. No, says Amazu. The quivering voices are the closest one gets to the human soul, to stirring emotions, a weeping without name or form. Bullshit, I tell him. Why should anything 'beautiful beyond measure' be explained as 'haunting'? 'Culture, my good friend,' says Amazu, 'you are uncultured.' Because I don't like people bellowing from torture chambers? But Amazu is a good host, so I tolerate his defence of things operatic.

We don't talk about much Desiree. Or maybe we do. Silently. There are times I admit to disliking her (hate is too strong a word), to acknowledging some of her sinister attributes. Only a single-minded cynic like her could manage to live without a display of emotions; in the same way a discarded shell says nothing of the snail that once dragged it around. I refuse to talk to Amazu about my imprisonment – about which he is most curious. He wants to know too many things: the meals, the effects of solitude, prison dreams, ways around erotic charges, how much of one's memory one can mine before madness sets in. He wants to know how one survives feelings of longing, manages time crawling past, endures unpredictable interrogations, knowing how they often lead to one's romance with the gallows. Which is worse: loss of freedom or fear of death? Which would I have chosen had I been granted a single wish? I have, of course, thought a lot about Amazu's questions in my time. But as things stand, in this house (that seems to have survived a nuclear blast) littered with mathematical puzzles, I politely deflect his probing with 'I have a lot on my mind'. But he is persistent. Do I have to now – I ask Amazu – reduce the charms and perils of existence to a single wish? Amazu laughs, says I would have done well as head of a school of philosophy some place, some time – only without the cynicism. I leave Amazu preparing to solve for *x*, his cogitations serenaded by a 'Pavarotti and Friends' recording.

Part of the problem, the reason for my unexpected, silent revolt, is my sudden awakening to the full gravity of Desiree's heartlessness. Amazu is puzzled by my apparent indifference to her, my lack of visible compassion for her condition. But Amazu does not understand what over two decades of incessant rebuff and brutal rebuke does to a heart, the smudges it leaves on the soul. We ruminate on these things; upon which he gently asks: 'What *do* brutal rebukes do to a heart, a soul?' I am moody and dismissive of his question, impatient with his relentless probing – a probing without purpose or accountability. 'Life is not mathematics,' I tell him, to which he responds that everything under the sun has a mathematical basis. The Great Wall of China. Military rations. Birth control pills. Of course he is a fanatic, a slave to numbers and theorems; yet there is a degree of truth to his claims.

But what does the chemical composition of birth control pills have to do with the fact that Desiree is a sadistic sociopath with a penchant for bullying and scheming? A ruthless chameleon with a methodical mind and a heart of stone? 'I don't believe in love,' she'd said, when what she really meant was she enjoyed teasing and baiting lovelorn souls; enjoyed watching how they writhed in tormented spasms of love, terrorised by her deliberate indecision. How do I explain all this to Amazu? How do I tell him that in a peculiar way, by a twisted kind of logic, it is better to have Desiree breathing through beeping machines than on her feet, brutalising souls?

But I, even when seething with helpless anger, know that none of my dim thoughts has any basis in lived reality. I also know that Amazu's mathematics is a futile topic for polite conversation. So we continue to suffer, Amazu and I, in our own separate and idiosyncratic ways. He sings opera, sinks his mind into myriad mathematical probabilities, while I take long walks in the company of Benito and my trumpet. How useless it is, this brass horn, silently collecting my saliva while I rearrange my soul, while my mind deadlocks on where my next meal is going to come from, wracked by the guilt of being parasite in Amazu's house. Not that Amazu ever complains; but I am assailed by the guilt nonetheless, driven to making up stories about why I cannot take meals with him, starve while food awaits. I invent excuses: imaginary stomach bugs, nausea, toothaches.

Still this does not stop me from imagining him secretly kicking cupboards and cursing under his breath, complaining to his humourless fellow mathematicians about the aspirant trumpeter-loafer in his house, who deprives the neighbours of sleep with his nocturnal ballads. Maybe he also tells them of my poetry recitals in the bath. Perhaps they laugh, choke on their peanut-butter sandwiches at his tales of how I loathe and love Desiree in equal measure. How I deny myself even the minutest satisfactions in life. How everything, for me, must come labelled: CONTAINS PURE MORAL INGREDIENTS. NO ARTIFICIAL COLOURANTS. Who is to say whether they, tired of solving mathematical puzzles, do not tell their wives and concubines about the drooling idiot who still believes in the triumph of the human spirit, in the rearrangement of ordained cosmic order? And if the wives and concubines don't tell their friends about me; the former prisoner who, after years of confinement, still refuses to say for which belief, which idea, he endured such suffering? Some will mutter in whispered sympathy, saying: 'Poor thing. Maybe deep down in his being he knows something we don't.' 'Yes,' their friends will mock them, 'what earth-shattering truths could possibly come from an embittered cynic who until now slept in city parks and mall restrooms? What wisdom could come from a drifting soul dislocated from its deceptions, its embedded conspiracy theories?

Most importantly,' they would opine, 'does he really matter?'

I continue with my walks to the Nelson Mandela Bridge, for a view of the cityscape, a glance into the faces of passing multitudes for whom freedom is a mockery of all things decent. A disease sweeps across the land. I cannot see an end to everyone wanting to be a Comrade Q. In certain ways, Comrade Q has ceased to be a mere ghost wielding influence, has become a force to be reckoned with. Eighteen years behind bars. For this? But how do I tell the multitudes that Comrade Q is, still, just a ghost, a shadow that lurks in overpriced private bars and exclusive hotels, in sprawling palatial homes and at fashionable funerals, in imported Mercedes Benzes with sonorous engine tones? And so, despairing, I watch from the side lines while the ghost wrecks our dreams. I call silently on the stars above to shake us from our heedless slumber, in beds soaked with the urine of orphans and the blood of slain men of goodwill. These musings, disturbing and draining, leave a bitter taste in my mouth.

My broodings continue at the Nelson Mandela Bridge; nothing in particular, just a collection of criss-crossing longings in no particular sequence or pattern. I am gnawed by a biting loneliness so severe that I wish, at times, I were dead. I know I am beyond feminine company – that no amount of romantic giggling and fleeting small talk will alter the path I have chosen: a winding one-way road to neurosis. I have resolved to play my trumpet, not for money, but as an honouring of my fledgling gift. It now makes no difference if coins are thrown at my feet, whether I am cursed, praised or loathed; for I have, in my trumpet-playing, touched the furthest nerve that holds what remains of my soul in place. That nerve, the appreciation of things both heart-warming and profane, is what makes bearable my time here. But I also know this sudden surrender to what is, this embracing of life's plagues, is more reluctant defeat than revelation of the meaning of existence; to which Amazu, when I share the thought, protests: 'Who says life has to mean something? What is a meaningful, exemplary life?' I have no answer, except to plead with him to accept sweaty coins earned from my trumpet sessions. My humble contribution to my upkeep.

Amazu returns home with a page of faded ink. A notice-board advertisement: 'Jazz trumpeter wanted, R2 000 per week. Must read and write music.' It is a generous offer, says Amazu. 'Plus, you get to do what you love. All you have to do is pick up the phone.' The prospect of being in the company of other musicians propels me to the phone on the kitchen wall. I dial:

011 307 0060. A hung-over, raspy voice contradicts everything written on the advert. It is a sort-of campus band, managed by session musicians off campus, he tells me. Yes, he is the band leader, and no, he cannot guarantee I will get paid. It all depends on the door takings. He adds, with an evil chuckle, that there are plenty of fringe benefits in being with the Lightning Bolts – the best Johannesburg band by far. I have never heard of the Lightning Bolts, I tell him. He is suddenly irritable; the judgement is immediate: 'You move in the wrong circles,' he says, and curtly adds: 'Are you in or out?' Music is a leap of faith, he tells me. 'There is no fucking around with decisions, my man, the clock is ticking.' 'What's your name?' I ask him, at which he sighs: 'Bradley fucking Jones; now are you in or out?' I am in, I tell him, but what are the fringe benefits? 'We are the resident gig at Club Rebel, so tits and free booze, dude; welcome to paradise.' Why would I want to be in a strip-club band, prostituting my art to horny soulless people? I would rather starve, I tell him, than sell my soul for money. To which he calmly says: 'Fuck you very much then and get starving,' and slams the phone down.

'And?' asks Amazu.

'Not a chance in hell. The guy is a nut case.'

'Sorry. Something better will come along,' says the ever-assuring Amazu.

Two nightmares continue to haunt me: I see myself walking up a rocky mountain tip, below which there is a raging sea. I slip on a loose rock and plunge head-first towards protruding rocks in the foamy waters below. I must have fallen hundreds of times off that same cliff, never cracking my skull open; just this sustained, eerie, sinking fall that leaves me drenched in sweat, my voice hoarse from screaming. Not that Amazu ever hears anything. He sleeps like a log. When not falling from cliffs, I dream I am walking across a vast desert, up and down treacherous sand dunes. I follow a caravan of naked nomads (old bearded men, young athletic boys) battling to outpace an approaching sandstorm. I grit the sand in my teeth, yell at the top of my voice after the convoy. No one looks back. They lead their camels on, oblivious to my fading screams, until the sandstorm swallows everything in sight.

Someone from the hospital phones. The message, delivered to a sleepy Amazu, is brief and devastating. I have never seen such consuming grief, so searing and paralysing that Amazu, telephone in hand, just freezes. He begins to tremble uncontrollably in shock and disbelief. He confirms what I already know: Desiree has died. My own grief is less immediate. It is that lingering, numb, silent type – repressed yet exploding in hidden minute detonations. Amazu says he will take a shower, as if to cleanse himself of the death news. I have not encountered many mourning people, so I find

121

myself out of my depth in consoling him; the more so because I have as yet not fully put logic and feeling to the news just received. I go over to him, place my hand on his shoulder. He does not acknowledge the hand, moves away like someone about to walk to the end of the universe yet too drained to manage even the first step. In the shower he sings; such captivating and mesmerising vocal variations, the skill of which leaves me humbled. Spurred by the tempo of shower water, soothed by steam, the singing rises and falls with precision – a driving urge to give a voice to pain. He must have emptied the whole geyser, cold water and all, for he emerges ashy and shivering. Strange. We were at the hospital less than a day ago. Desiree, though evidently not of this world, gave no indication of deciding to become a permanent corpse. We expected that day would come – but knew little how sudden and catastrophic it would be.

We are too stunned to eat, to think, or make sense of anything. Amazu returns from his bedroom perfumed, his bulky self wrapped in a cream evening gown. Something is amiss. There is a sudden unfriendliness about him, a seething moodiness. To warm the frosty demeanour, I suggest we go to the hospital either now or first thing in the morning; Desiree's next-of-kin paperwork. He does not answer but continues to pace about the house, picking up and throwing things around, searching. In silence he turns couch pillows upside down, moves furniture and peers underneath it, packs and unpacks newspaper stacks in quick, sweeping motions. He begins to sweat, the frostiness replaced by visible anger; anger that soon grows into hisses, then bursting rage. 'I was *this* close –' he demonstrates with his index finger and thumb, '*this* close! Why don't you have respect for other people's things? I told you to leave everything as you found it, just the way it was, no matter how dirty you judged it to be. How hard is that? There is greatness in this mess! Why do you insist on changing things that don't belong to you?'

I always suspected that Amazu was the kind of man you ran to when life dealt you evil cards, but that his generosity hid a failure battling to redeem himself. That despite his temporary offers of sanctuary, he would always be a predictable disappointment. Burdened by the news of Desiree's demise, the helplessness of my homelessness (how quickly the hesitant body gets used to other people's beds), all I can do is ask what sin I had committed to warrant such grandstanding and abuse. The crime, as I soon learn, is in having moved the yellowing newspapers, swarming with ants and pizza crumbs, from the couches into the dustbin – from there (today being Friday) to be ground under the crushing blades of municipal refuse removal trucks. The yellowing newspaper, says my accuser, had scribbled on it the closest, most elaborate and refined mathematical formula that proved beyond a shadow of a doubt that life is meaningless. Everyone solves for x, the unknown. Mathematically, you can calculate all the way to your grave; someone, somewhere, is bound to disprove your hard-earned insights, create new problems and confusions along the way. Meaninglessness is impossible to reduce to a single formula. I feel sorry for Amazu. Such passion, such relentless, disjointed inquiry, noted on newspapers, milk cartons and pizza boxes.

The fact that Amazu is so serious, that he does not even pause for breath, means only one thing: Amazu Ogbedo believes his theory. I find the entire episode depressingly sad but at the same time hilarious. I break out into muted laughter that soon gives way to a wave of howling gasps that leaves my head pounding, my ribs sore. I completely lose my composure, forced to keep laughing even when I desperately want to stop. My laughter – dangerous laughter – only worsens Amazu's anger. Unhinged by the news of his lover's death, enraged by the loss of the greatest mathematical formula ever calculated, he walks past me to the front door which he holds open and, in the most polite manner, says: 'Please leave my home.' Not house; home.

I have no luggage to pack. All I have to do is fetch my trumpet and retrieve the dog from the indoor kennel, say my profound thanks and face the persistence of my vagabond life; the impending implosion of a brittle existence. The phone rings. Amazu ignores it while I, trumpet case in hand, go in search of Benito. The caller is persistent. Some eleven attempts later, he finally picks up: 'Amazu.' The conversation is brief, the effect immediate. There has been a terrible confusion, an unfortunate misunderstanding. Amazu clasps his hands together, unable to contain his joy. It was Desiree's ward mate who died, from surgical complications. A computer error. Our Desiree is still very much barely alive, continues to lie staring into space, her once-vibrant beauty daily eroded by time and disease.

Once broken ('Please leave my home'), some things can never be fixed. It does not help that my views on Amazu have always been muddled, never quite settled. I am grateful for the guaranteed meals and hot showers – yet remind him that it was never my intention to abide with him for eternity. There is no doubt that, thanks to him, I am well fed, no longer the gaunt corpse that entered 184 Jan Smuts Avenue six months earlier. The regular baths and grooming have somewhat lifted my spirits, though I cannot deny that the yoke of advancing age reminds me of my imminent collapse. You cannot be a vagabond forever, the yoke says. So I suffer blinding headaches, my joints creak and my mouth is often salty.

Apart from those afflictions, there are the humiliating accidents of an unreliable bladder, not to mention bowels that seem so erratic that I never know when I will need to sprint for the bathroom – only to be further embarrassed by the squeaky meows of bowels in turmoil. If breaking wind were an elixir, I would be the healthiest soul in the southern hemisphere. There is also the problem of memory: I say and do things with good intent, only to be stunned by tearful gratitude or rebukes, days later. It is peculiar, and disconcerting, how I often wake irritable and upset, yet unable to remember the reason for my sullen mood. Amazu knew how to deflate my wanton feelings of anger (like dogs snapping at hands that pull them by the tail), by saying pedantically: 'There are many kinds of suffering in the world. Some are self inflicted.' I envied his barren analysis of life, hated his matter-of-fact views on things requiring feeling; loathed his manner of living, his mathematical existence.

In reality, I tell Amazu, my going has little to do with the fact that he explicitly kicked me out of his home and more to do with me breathing freely under Johannesburg's tempestuous skylines. Observing the little things: beggars pulling shopping trolleys filled with all manner of useless possessions; the trusting pigeons pecking at bread crumbs in my palm; shadows rising and falling as the sun scorches the clouds brewing rain.

I walk out into the sweltering heat – no destination in mind. Along Jan Smuts Avenue the traffic crawls, the numerous luxury automobiles making it clear that there is a world within a world: two Johannesburgs – one for vagabonds and the other for senior executives speaking animatedly into smart phones while cruising in Mercedes Benzes as big as boats. In this other Johannesburg, the one of plush, air-conditioned cars, the revolution is without the slightest meaning. The executives collect revolution memorabilia on the struggle: coffee-table books and BBC documentaries. But their lives are no struggle. They simply throw money at things. Uncomplicated. Benito whimpers, sniffs my heels as we walk purposelessly towards Oxford Road, past Rosebank, towards Melrose.

Johannesburg thunderheads hint at the possibility of rain. I, hungry dog in hand, trumpet slung on my right shoulder, walk in the afternoon sun. Where could I possibly go to avoid the coming storm, if not to loiter around, looking suspicious? Corlett Drive takes me past unremarkable sights, the occasional belch of diesel smoke from construction trucks and metro buses. I walk downhill, weak at the knees, freed from Amazu's generosity, his silent judgements. Blue lights flash in the distance. I see police frisking people, lining them up against walls. An impromptu detour, an early right turn, lands me at Melrose Arch, passing beautiful women throwing their heads back in staged laughter. Bentleys and Lamborghinis are parked in front of the Melrose Arch Hotel, friends, lovers and sophisticated thieves dining at sidewalk restaurants. Someone picks guitar strings (acoustic) in the hotel lobby. He is not trying to milk money from people; he is making his playing exactly that: playing. He plays to create mood, a receptive ambience, and can be instructed to stop any time the hotel management deems fit. Through the revolving doors I see him grinning and nodding to passing guests dragging their bags on wheels; casually tuning and retuning his instrument amid the courteous applause from those resting on the reception couches. Youngish good looks, well-tailored grey suit. How do I tell him: on my shoulder is a trumpet, ready to accompany your strings? How do I say to him: take a bow, rest, go for a walk, meet the daughters of famous fund managers? Envy eats at me. I imagine the prospects: trumpeting in an air-conditioned hotel lobby for a set salary! How receptive his audience is, knowing nothing is expected of them but to sip good wine, free from moral obligations.

A man, unbeknown to me, observes me from an outdoor restaurant. He, moments later, walks towards me, taps my shoulder, offers me a handshake. 'Couldn't help noticing,' he says. 'Francois de Wet. Just thought I could be of assistance.' I am stung. What he means is, this is not a place for vagabonds, craning their necks into hotel lobbies, spying on strangers. Your dog, he wants to say, is sure to offend my patrons who have escaped the drudgery of less plush Johannesburg social nests to come and dine in peace. Don't you see you don't belong here? This is what he wants to say. I, not seeking pity, tell him my story without passion or emotion, acknowledging that it is possible that my very existence will offend some people here. And what's more, with a dog in tow, amidst dining places. I was not even intentionally coming to Melrose Arch, I tell him, it just happened. Will I blame him if he thinks I am a bloodsucker in search of hand-outs? I compliment his well-trimmed moustache, joke that it reminds me of famous writers.

He is a leech, sucking me for clues so as to dissect me and hang my remains in public squares to hisses of: vagabond! My bowels growl, an embarrassing, needy growl, a growl of famine.

But I am wrong about Francois de Wet. The manager-owner of Café Mesopotamia, eleven years strong, he is no stranger to hardship himself. Thrice divorced, with grown children, the girl a commercial pilot and the son a recovering drug addict, paralysed in a motorcycle accident. 'I am short of waiters; if it's something you want to consider ...' he says. I thank him for his kindness, and we walk past dining exhibitionists into his modest office. He gives me a form, dials a number, requests two plates of lamb shank, for Benito and I. Legitimate guests! He lays out the road ahead: an introduction to Café Mesopotamia menus, three weeks' training (difficult customers, wine lists, Café Mesopotamia etiquette), and 'many other things as we go along'. I notice photos on the desk; there they are, the pilot and the drug addict. But not a single picture of wives past. I eat like a runaway slave.

There is a twist to my good fortune: I need, having completed the forms, to finalise everything with Tony, a tattooed giant impatiently clapping hands, sending waiters jetting in all directions: 'Table 2, Mandy. Move!' 'Come Fred, keep them coming. You forgot lemon slices for Mr Douglas.' 'There you are Celeste. Happy birthday sweetheart, but you are fucking up my orders today.' Celeste is offended – the way she smiles with her teeth only, the small pouchy

129

mouth trained to suppress revolt. Speed. Precision. Hippopotamus-hide-thick temperament, in defence of the Café Mesopotamia reputation.

What is Tony going to say to me? I am getting tired of your leaking bladder, old man, go tend tomato plants and leave my tables alone? Put that fucking trumpet away before I impale you with it? Are there no lesser demands: dishes, floor-mopping, bar-associated errands? I shudder to think what awaits me. But when did things get so fast, where one is not even permitted a moment to think about the task at hand? Is eighteen years that long, that existence seems to be turned on its head? Or is it aftershocks of prison life that have slowed me, all those weeks in solitary confinement when it mattered not whether time moved or didn't? Everyone in this city seems programmed to be in a hurry, to hop on the speed train to nowhere. Benito licks his plate clean.

Francois bids me farewell (the daughter's wedding meeting), welcoming me to Café Mesopotamia in advance. On my way out, walking past animated conversations bathed in self-indulgent laughter, I am confronted by a furious biker (long, curly black hair, leather pants and jacket): 'Hey! That's Raisin. That's my dog. Hey mister – have you any idea what you have put me through, stealing my dog? Dog thief!' He yanks the dog from my embrace, full of hostile intent. Numerous pairs of condemning eyes cut me to shreds, before forks and knives resume slicing pork and whatever else on multiple plates. All these faces, chewing gum, smiling into cellphones, getting kissed.

Who are these catastrophically stupid, soul-deprived people dining in hordes?

The biker, Benito firmly in his hold, strides to a Harley Davidson parked nearby. He fires the engine, and with an explosive rumble, Benito disappears into the afternoon sun. I am a welter of emotions: Shocked. Embarrassed. Offended. A woman exits Club Kilimanjaro, offers to walk me 'wherever you are going'. We head back along Corlett Drive. She is thirty or so, maybe older, wears tight jeans and a floral blouse. Her make-up boasts all sorts of precisions: eye liner, mascara, lascivious lips painted an oppressive red. A beautiful, younger version of herself lurks somewhere inside her; a self far from the schemer that pursues me.

'I saw you with Francois. He is a nice man.'

'Yes.'

'Can I interest you in some pleasure? I am Catherine. But friends call me Brutal Kate.'

'I am not interested in pleasure,' I protest.

'I don't sell my vagina, if that's what you think. You can get that from your wife. I sell the mysterious. I make lewdness possible.'

'I don't care if you sell space rockets. I am not interested.'

'It is not only pleasure; I expose you to other worlds.'

I snap at her: 'Have I asked to be exposed to other worlds? Stop following me, please!' Her face contorts, works itself into a confrontational mask: 'Timid old shit – choke on your miserable life!' she spits. I ignore her and quicken my pace, leaving her sulking and dejected. My thoughts are with my dog friend, so callously taken from me, without any discussion. I walk back to 184 Jan Smuts Avenue, to negotiate a few more nights under Amazu's roof.

Tony is, as I have predicted, unpleasant. My training at Café Mesopotamia starts at dawn, and ends after midnight on most days. The demands of the wealthy, existing in a bubble of their own, are worse than the occasional rude remarks I endured at Mary Fitzgerald Square. It seems to me that the patrons' nights out have little to do with eating, and much to do with showing off expensive cars and promiscuous lovers. I have trouble remembering orders (they sound to me like insolent instructions), even when I write them down. My shifts are gloomy, polluted by irritable remarks and 'call your manager' ultimatums. It is not unusual to hear a patron explode: 'Are you deaf? I said absolutely no pork!' 'Strawberry milkshake is not the same as a tot of vodka – she's eight years old, for crying out loud!' 'I said well done for my lamb chops – three times – why are you serving me raw, bloody meat? Do I look like a vampire to you?' I am not like Celeste, skilled in silent revolt. My suppressed temper leaves a bitter taste in my mouth, the more so because such lapses mean I have to answer to a raving Tony, bent on chewing me up alive. Francois de Wet offers no protection.

14

The dark figure is, after years on the run, finally arrested on charges of multiple murder. He refuses a lawyer, and sits through an eleven-month trial without raising so much as a whisper in his own defence. The newspapers soon coin a name for him: The Silent Terror. He finally pleads temporary insanity when confronted by twelve life sentences, citing manic-depressive behaviour resulting from grief and mourning for his beloved uncle, mistakenly shot dead by police on suspicion of drug trafficking. His arrest and subsequent conviction brings me no relief from my persistent angst.

Amazu and I watch the trial on his black and white television: the legal wrangles, the conflicting interpretations of grades of madness, the burden on the state to prove beyond reasonable doubt that The Silent Terror is a sadistic killer. With his future looking gloomier than the fires of hell, he hangs himself on Christmas Day. News crews capture moving shots of distraught families weeping on the steps of the Supreme Court at answers denied them by the troubled young man with beautiful teeth. 'Psychotic coward,' despairs Amazu. 'Maybe not,' I tell him.

The Sphinx greets you at the Café Mesopotamia entrance. You are led by an archway through crimson walls guarded by Pharaohs. The floor is decorated with an assortment of hieroglyphics, anything from lone eyes to people with animal heads. The passage to the bar is a simulation of the Nile, with water pumped under the walkway to create an impression of dining over a river. Café Mesopotamia service awards are mounted on scrolls tinged with gold and blood-red detail, doubling as wall art. The private dining suite, two floors under the restaurant, is the most expensive. It is adorned with plush furniture and terraced seating, surrounded by pictures of famous people photographed next to the pyramids, with Egyptian locals leading their camels across vast landscapes.

Unlike the other waitrons, I find waiting tables wounding work. 'This is the service industry,' Nico barks at me, 'you have to put your heart in it.' Hard as I try, I find I cannot accustom myself to the monotony of perpetually grinning into the faces of strangers, feigning interest in their self-indulgent stories. There is this aura of self-importance about them, an arrogant expectation that disregards the wishes of others. Life's absurdities continue: Ms Tobin and her religious friends frequent our bar, on 'girls' nights out'. A touch of shame washes over me as she watches me running around with steaming plates, wiping ice cream off spoiled brats, waiting on diners discussing French perfumes instead of ordering their meals. The look in her eyes is one that I read as relief and pity; until she, weeks later, calls me to Table 6, reaches into her handbag, and hands me three letters. She had to open them, she confesses, couldn't contain her curiosity. I am both annoyed and grateful, and smile in the way only an annoyed, grateful waiter should. My entire library sustained irreparable water damage, she tells me, so bad, the books all had to be thrown away. The poetry notebooks, too. Ms Tobin confesses to reading the poetry to her book club and, as if to redeem herself for her prying eyes, says: 'We all agree you are immensely gifted. Look on the bright side: you don't have to pay storage fees anymore.' I feel numb.

The handwriting on the letters is unmistakable: Mercedes. Gabriel, she tells me in the first short letter, has been in and out of hospital for a while now. He lost the sight in his left eye. He sits under a mulberry tree listening to a small transistor radio, sulking at everything and everyone. There are times when she feels wronged by his ingratitude, his aged cynicism. The second letter is no different from the first: hospital visits, the sulks under the tree, more hospital visits – culminating in a brief intensive-care stint resulting from a mild diabetic stroke. Gabriel is far from a saint, she says, goes on to describe the philandering ways of the younger Gabriel, a romantic whirlwind who charmed the hearts of female fellow journalists. It was well known that Gabriel used his desk at the newsroom as one indiscriminate bed. Colleagues caught him in compromising situations, whereby he, for years, claimed 'journalistic research' to mask his wayward ways. In truth, Rosaline Sanchez and Rafael Lopez were childhood friends, and if fate were fair, Rosaline should have married Rafael; were it not for Gabriel's elaborate promises. In other words, if there were anyone most qualified to violate Gabriel's marriage, it was none other than Rafael Lopez who, witnessing Rosaline's drift into despair, availed a cushioned shoulder to cry on. The murder was more the result of blind rage than righteous anger, and the guilt that still chips away at Gabriel's heart has its roots in belated regret. It was when confronted with the stiffening corpse of Rafael that Gabriel discovered he knew not who he was – a realisation that continues to plague him. 'Why are you so quiet? Are you not getting my letters? Anyway, Dad has become something of a ghost, sitting under a tree poking the ground with his walking stick. He refuses to see any of his friends or family – just sits there, muttering to himself.'

Her third letter opens with a shock: 'Dad died two weeks ago. We found him sitting under the tree with his radio as usual, his walking stick on his lap. It was a mongrel licking his fingers that alerted me that something was amiss. Ambulance staff confirmed he had been dead for several hours. We buried him with his reporter awards in a private family ceremony. All his siblings came, despite their fiery exchanges before his passing.

'It was a moving ceremony – more so because Carlos,

our local pastor, who is Rafael's twin brother, officiated at the burial. That is all I have to say about my father. As for me? I am holding on. I have stopped music altogether. I now weave baskets at the local art centre, a hobby I started as a way to escape my father. The weaving hurts your fingers at first, but you soon get used to it. The baskets cost about fifty pesos each. We are a group of six women, two from Costa Rica, three from Las Tunas, the other from Santiago de Cuba. It's a sisterhood. You should have come here. You would have loved Cuba and its contradictions – our outdated American cars, desperate people dying, drowning en route to becoming Cuban Americans. Fleeing from a revolution that yielded small things: aging sugar-cane plantations and rum distilleries. Socialism. Phew! Raúl Castro is rumoured to be next in line. Fidel is old and sickly. Our friend Benito is back here from New York. He is distant these days, indifferent. He returned home with a woman. Isabeau. A French girl.

'I see some disturbing news about South Africa in the press. The pockets of greed. But that is the nature of revolutions. They all have discomforts. Disappointments. Anyway, I have to go, my poet. Please, please, please ... write. Love, Mercedes.'

I raise my eyes from the letter to find Tony staring coldly at me: 'Table 14 has been waiting for cutlery since the Dark Ages.' But I am too distracted to take offence; I fold the letter and, with a nod, say: 'Cutlery with the speed of light to Table 14.'

Amazu loves the food parcels I bring home: Mutton

curry. Puddings. Fish dishes. He licks his fingers in the evenings, says God works in mysterious ways. Life continues at 184 Jan Smuts Avenue; Amazu, Algebra the cat and I.

I am nervous about writing to Mercedes. What if I sound dejected, desperate? What do I say, now that she has undergone such eerie transformation – a music teacher turned weaver of baskets? The photograph, enclosed in her last letter, screams the loudest change: a daughter frustrated by her father's distance, finding solace in food, becoming a chubby weaver of baskets with expressionless eyes.

The decision not to write to Mercedes bothers me. I confuse orders, forget basic waiter courtesies, sulk at justified patron protests. I am appalled by the speed of my aging: one day you stride along Sophiatown streets, confident in the abundance of life, the next you wake with a fast-greying head and deep question-mark furrows on the sides of your mouth. You acquire a permanent frown not consistent with the natural purpose of frowns – a reflex expressive of permanent inherent angst. You listen to drunken young women confessing atrocious tragedies at the hands of sugar daddies, weeping in your aging arms simply because they have nowhere else to go. You wake to a sudden loss of lust, confronted by polished and perfumed young things with hypnotic curves and see-through blouses (nipples like freshly picked strawberries) – while you continue with the routine of mopping floors, running around with vegetable soups and smoked salmon. You forget how to submit to urges. You are suddenly engrossed with remembering and misremembering things past, rearranging them in different sequence, in futile attempt to rid over-familiar tragedies of their sting.

I feel a rebellious impulse to rid Café Mesopotamia of its abusive sugar-daddy contingent – a resolve not appreciated by ungrateful female youth: 'You are not my father!' they protest. Suddenly, sadly, experience of the world means nothing. The message is clear: keep your knowledge to yourself. We will, if we so decide, come ask for your opinion, but not otherwise; for in these times, our times, there is no such thing as decency. So I mutter to myself, at the helplessness of it all: fifteen-year-olds blowing smoke rings on the laps of potbellied sugar daddies; wealthy spinsters on the prowl for lazy school-leaver boys with reliable erections; Comrade Q clones sipping imported whisky at the Café Mesopotamia bar. To think I buried paupers, dug potatoes with my bare hands, suffered haunting hallucinations, only to be dismissed with an old refrain: 'This is Johannesburg.'

It is a hot afternoon. I decline to accompany Amazu to the hospital to see Desiree. I, when not ferrying pork ribs and salami salads, continue with my walks to the Nelson Mandela Bridge. I lean on the bridge railing, admire sun rays bouncing off railway lines. You can smell the greasy residue after each passing train, moving souls from one promise to the other, from one heartbreak to the next. There is, by late evening (except for moths waltzing in the evening light), a spooky calm that descends on the city; funeral-procession kind of calm. A stray cat crosses railway lines below, followed by a slowing train grinding to a halt, its lit windows like houses in motion. A group of young men approach from both ends of the bridge, sandwiching me between them. Hyenas. Hunting in packs. I sense trouble but shake off the feeling.

It is becoming increasingly tempting to jump off the bridge onto the approaching trains below – to be electrocuted to soot, roasted to a charred thing, unrecognisable even to pathologists. I have my reasons, estimations and convictions for wanting to end this nightmare, but I sense I am yet to discover something profound. Something small. That holds all the big things together. An aquarium of sorts, where I could look in, see meaning swimming around coral reeds, in pinks and fiery reds. An aquarium with a hole at the top, to allow a hand to plunge into the clear water, grab the meaning in a tight clasp, show it to all: Desiree, Amazu, Ms Tobin, Gabriel and Mercedes Sanchez – to everyone – and say: I did not suffer for nothing. Here, in the palm of my hand, is the reward! Here – see it? Touch it if you want, but be sure to put it back into the water.

Life, I think to myself, is held together by small things. Much like Amazu's theorems, written on newspapers and fermenting milk cartons. The young men walk past. I eavesdrop, hear something about the booming abortion trade in Hillbrow and downtown Johannesburg: pills, wire, industrial detergents. One says something about Saddam Hussein fished from a hole in Tikrit.

Echoes

15

I, at the back of my mind, always knew I would one day walk away from Café Mesopotamia, away from Amazu, away from the once-radiant Desiree, now covered in bedsores. I will maybe dig a hole, a grave in which to wait for real dying – whenever it decides to come. A storm brews. I walk for days along Beyers Naudé Drive, in search of a mountainous retreat, past settlements and farms. I follow criss-crossing footpaths into the mountains, past chirping birds and the occasional lizard. I have few expectations: to find a desolate mountain, see what awaits there. An outline of the Johannesburg skyline can be seen in the distance, skyscrapers reaching out to the furious black clouds. I climb over boulders, dodge thorns and spider webs, until I reach a ravine, hidden at the foot of a mountain.

I arrive at a secluded cliff at midnight, amid a heavy, windy downpour. It is as if thousands of waterfalls have suddenly been let loose from some faraway planet. Below is a neglected caravan. The rainwater has washed the caravan, exposing rusted and stained windows (greased with child palm prints). The caravan door is ajar, the wind blowing water through the doorway. It stands askew, sinking further with each passing day, the rubber on its tyres exposing rusted wire, its walls used as chalkboards. Daring drawings. Done in soot. An old shoe, without a heel, is under the bed, amid wet cigarette butts. On the wall next to the cracked window is a crooked nail, on which hangs a stringless, unloved acoustic guitar. The wardrobe doors are off the hinges, their backs used as havens for the imagination.

A child's hand has, in purple ink, drawn a wheelless car; trees floating over sea or river water; a plate stacked with food. One of the wardrobe drawers hides an abandoned comb, a child's milk bottle (with faded measurements), a broken typewriter. On the bed are old steelwool-like blankets, a rock-hard pillow, punctuated with bread crumbs. The rain continues to pour with determined fury, the wind howls past. The trees beam with each lightning bolt. I am thirsty. I extend the baby's milk bottle, rinse it, wait for it to fill. The water is cold, settles my edgy mood. The window is stuck in rust and dirt, stays open to winds and flying sand. I lower myself onto the soaked bed, lying on my back. Someone lives here. But who?

The view is of expansive landscape, untouched by greedy developers, where plants still tease the nostrils with their natural scents. There are times when I get nervous, edgy, when my senses warn me of fast-advancing danger ... which never comes. There is the lurking risk of snake and scorpion bites. Just above the abandoned caravan are boulders surrounded by shrubs, next to which is a cave. There is no freer feeling than sitting on the highest stone ledge overlooking the valley and blowing the trumpet amid startled lizards and cautious birds. I point the trumpet into the valley below, play meditative tunes – to heart-warming response from echoes that seem to emerge from God Himself. There is a peculiar harmony in listening to the valley mimic my horn, an overwhelming sense of existence in the company of rabbits and falcons.

Gushes of rainwater have carved a well on one of the stones inside the small cave. Crawling in on all fours, I am able to reach the cool water protected from dust and other pollutants. The water doubles as a mirror. I cringe at my unkempt hair, my biblical-prophet beard. Hunger pangs have taught me to stone small game with admirable precision; to bury my meat (covered in leaves) deep in the river sand (a stream, really) next to the caravan, ensure it stays there by rolling a boulder over it. The cave is also a sanctuary for keeping the remains of fire going (to avoid resorting to caveman ways every time fire is needed). I, when not searching for stray fish in shallow swamps, when not practising the trumpet, when not searching for guinea fowl eggs, when not hiding from helicopters roaring past, when not spellbound by the various moon phases, not twisted into an agonised ball from suspect meat, not filing my nails on rocks, not mistaking rock stains for San rock art, not waking from a dream wherein I lowered the panties of a charming stranger, not designing fishing and hunting tools, steaming or freezing from fevers, overwhelmed by sudden waves of raging anger, rolling

with bursts of rib-bending laughter at odd things, or
writing poetry on mud, still think Desiree is the only
soul for whom my heart throbbed.

There is no telling how all this will end, if someone
will one day stumble upon a decomposing corpse, or
whitened bones licked clean by rain and jackals. There
is no telling what hikers will make of the abandoned
caravan, my hammock designed from reeds and grass,
the eternal silence only death can bring. They will
maybe kick the rusted trumpet, frown at how it got
here in the first place. They will never know, not in the
truest sense, that the greasy corpse or the white bones
belonged to a dreamer, an average man overtaken by
fate. They will make nothing of the caravan, never
know that yet another recluse preceded me, leaving
behind a one-string guitar. They will photograph the
setting sun in passing, and never get to befriend the
pleasing moon that hangs over the valley like a giant
orange, never stay long enough to tell the moon their
thoughts, their discoveries, their secrets. They will
rush back, to the trappings of Johannesburg, to Café
Mesopotamia, to pork ribs on decorated plates ferried
by wounded souls. I will not be there to tell them:
this rusty trumpet, you fools, is freedom. To certain
inconclusive degrees, I would tell them, these whitened
bones, charred by the sun, are as close as you are ever
going to get to meaning. As for my story – from the
dusty streets of Sophiatown to the rusty trumpet at
your feet – it is the story of a life of loss. Everything.
But that is not the sad part. The bewildering thing
about it all is how many stories, some worse than
mine, lurk in the shadows. Bees, I would tell them.

Not a gunshot. Not a hangman's noose. Not double pneumonia. Not hunger nor a brutalised heart. I was killed by bees. Small things.

One last thing: I forgot to tell you my name. On second thoughts, never mind.